THEA: A VAMPIRE STORY

BOOK 1

STEVEN JENKINS

THEA: A VAMPIRE STORY
Copyright © 2016 by Steven Jenkins

The right of Steven Jenkins to be identified as the author of the Work has been asserted to him in accordance with the Copyright, Designs and Patents Act 1988.

Published in Great Britain in 2016 by Different Cloud Publishing.

"For Granddad."

CONTENTS

Free Books   vii

PART I
INTO THE FIRE
Chapter 1   3
Chapter 2   7
Chapter 3   16

PART II
TEENAGE KICKS
Chapter 4   25
Chapter 5   32
Chapter 6   35

PART III
FAMILY BLOOD
Chapter 7   41
Chapter 8   50
Chapter 9   62
Chapter 10   69
Chapter 11   77
Chapter 12   84
Chapter 13   91
Chapter 14   99

PART IV
THICKER THAN WATER
Chapter 15   117
Chapter 16   124
Chapter 17   130

Chapter 18   135

PART V
BLACK SUN
Chapter 19   147
Chapter 20   152
Chapter 21   163
Chapter 22   167
Chapter 23   176

Also Available - Thea II: A Vampire Story   205
Free Books   207
Also Available - Blue Skin: Book One   209
Also Available - Eyes On You: A Ghost Story   211
Also Available - Burn The Dead: Quarantine   213
Also Available - Burn The Dead: Purge   215
Also Available - Burn The Dead: Riot   217
Also Available - Fourteen Days: A Ghost   219
Story
Also Available - Spine: A Collection of   221
Twisted Tales
Also Available - Rotten Bodies: A Zombie   223
Short Story Collection
About the Author   225

FREE BOOKS

For a limited time, you can download FREE copies of *Spine, Burn The Dead: Book 1 & Book 2* - The No.1 bestsellers from Steven Jenkins.

Available at: www.steven-jenkins.com

PART I

INTO THE FIRE

1

I *hear crying.*

My head shoots up from the pillow and I scurry out of bed. My first instinct is to go to Thea. I race over to her cot, lean over the railing and find her sleeping soundly, undisturbed.

It's coming from Ivy's room.

Normally, a crying child is commonplace this time of night. But things have definitely got worse since Mark walked out. I burst into Ivy's room, tripping over one of the many toys scattered across the floor. When I switch the light on, I see my little girl sitting up in bed, her face bright red from anguish. "Mummy's here, sweetheart," I say softly as I race over to her. I hate to see her cry—yet I cherish these moments of comfort the most. Sitting on the edge of the mattress, I stroke her long blonde hair. "Another nightmare?"

Ivy nods her head, sniffing loudly, her tears muting a little with just my presence.

"What was it about?" I ask.

Ivy looks at me with those pitiful blue eyes, that look she used to give when she knew she was in trouble. It always makes me smile inside, but saddens me at the same time. How could she ever be afraid of me? I would never hurt my girls. Nor would I allow anyone else. They're my angels. And it's my job to keep them safe.

"Come on, sweetheart," I say, "you can tell me? Was it about vampires again?"

Ivy nods again, wiping her eyes with the sleeve of her pink pyjamas. "They were everywhere," she replies, tugging on the quilt. "They were trying to eat me."

"It was only a dream. Vampires can't get you. They're extinct. Like dinosaurs. And you're not afraid of dinosaurs, are you?"

She shakes her head.

"*See?*" I say. "So just try not to think about them, okay?"

"But Mrs Rogers said that they still live in some parts of the world."

That bloody teacher. "Yes," I say with reluctance. "A few, I suppose. But not like the ones from hundreds of years ago. You'll never meet one. I'm an adult, and *I* haven't seen one. So there's no need to worry."

"Is it true that if you drink vampire blood, you turn into one?"

"Look, sweetheart, try not to think about it now. You need your sleep; you're a growing girl."

"Tracy Jones says that you become a slave."

"What are you talking about? A slave to who?"

"A slave to the vampire that *gave you* the blood."

I chuckle. "Tracy Jones is just teasing you. There's no such thing as a vampire slave."

Ivy looks unconvinced. I don't blame her though. Learning about vampires used to scare the hell out of me too. I wish they wouldn't teach it in schools. Not at eight-years-old, anyway. She's way too young. She should be learning about the wonderful things that exist in the world. *Not bloody monsters.* "Now, do you think you can get back to sleep?"

I smile when Ivy shrugs her shoulders because I know exactly what she's gunning for. "So what will make you go to sleep?" I ask.

"Sleep in your bed?" she replies with a cheeky grin.

There it is. Right on cue.

"Okay." *I'm a pushover.* "But just for tonight. In your own bed tomorrow."

"All right, Mum," she says, reaching forward to wrap her arms around me.

I pick her up off the bed, struggling with her weight. She's getting bigger. I suppose she was due a growth spurt. Maybe she'll be tall like her father.

Let's hope that's *all* she gets from that wanker.

2

It's finally over.

After almost five years of hell, that *prick* has broken Ivy's heart. The last thing I want is to see my little girl in so much pain, but I can't help but feel relieved. Callum was a worthless parasite; she's better off without him. What the hell did he ever do for her? *Apart from get a fifteen-year-old pregnant. And get her hooked on every substance under the sun.* He was never there for her. *I* was the one who took her to rehab. *I* was the one who was by her side when she had the abortion. *Me.* And where was Callum? Getting *fucked up* in some grotty flat, not even knowing what *day* it was.

Good riddance!

Ivy's hurting now. Of course she is—she's eighteen. But she'll get over him. It may take some time, but Thea and I will help her through it. That's what families are for.

She's been in her bedroom for three days now, and she's barely had a thing to eat. She says she's been clean for six months. I want to trust her, *I really do*, but it's hard. I've been let down so many times in the past. All I can do is keep an eye on her. And now that my baby's home, that's exactly what I'll do.

I leave the bathroom and see Thea standing outside her sister's bedroom.

"Ivy," she calls out, gently tapping on the door, "can I come in?"

"Go away!" I hear Ivy shout from inside.

"Do you want to watch *Ghostbusters* with me?" Thea asks. "It's your favourite." She's persistent; I'll give her that. But she's only ten years old. She's too young to understand what it's like to have your heart broken.

She will though.

"Leave me alone!" Ivy screams as something thuds against the door. Thea moves away in fright— I can't tell if it was a fist or a shoe—but either way, that girl is not ready to come out.

I walk over to Thea, her eyes filling up with tears, and then take her by the hand. "Come on, sweetheart," I say to her gently, "just give her a few more days. She's still hurting."

"She's been in there for so long though," Thea says, wiping her eyes. "Can't you talk to her?"

I steer her away from the door and down the stairs. "I've tried talking," I reply. "She just needs a little space."

"But I really miss her. *It's not fair.*"

"I know," I say as we walk into the living room, "but we have to be patient. I'll watch *Ghostbusters* with you instead. How does that sound?"

Thea sniffs, wiping her eyes again. "Okay, Mum."

"And how about I make us a nice hot chocolate?" I ask, leaning against the doorframe.

Smiling, she sits on the couch. "With marsh-mallows?"

"Okay, honey. I'll see if there's any left in the cupboard."

"Thanks, Mum."

Thea is beside me on the couch, curled up like a sleeping kitten. She only lasted about a half hour into the film before dozing off. Once she devoured her hot chocolate that was it. I love it when she falls asleep on the couch, or in the car. I can't exactly carry her to bed anymore, but the sight of it still warms my heart.

I could murder a glass of wine. *Or a bottle.* Hot chocolate is nice, but it's Saturday night. And it's been a tough few days with Ivy, so a glass of red would have gone down a treat. But I could never risk drinking in front of her. I couldn't bear to see another relapse. My angel's fought so hard for so long; it's the last thing she needs to see.

I turn to Thea and give her shoulder a gentle tap. "Wake up, sweetheart," I whisper. "Time for bed."

She starts to stir, her eyes half-opening. "What time is it?" she asks, drowsily.

I get up off the couch. "It's late. Way past your bedtime."

Rubbing her eyes, she yawns and then holds out both her hands. I grab them and pull her up.

Like a sleepwalker, she follows me out of the living room and up the stairs.

"Are we still going swimming tomorrow?" Thea asks as we pass Ivy's bedroom.

"Yes."

"Do you think Ivy will come with us?"

I glance at Ivy's closed door. "I doubt it. Maybe next week—when she's feeling better."

Thea tuts as we walk into her bedroom. Climbing under her pink quilt, Thea smiles at me and closes her eyes the moment her head hits the pillow. "Goodnight, Mum," she slurs. "See you tomorrow."

"Goodnight, sweetheart." I kiss her on the forehead and then softly stroke her soft blonde hair. "I love you."

"I love you, too."

No matter how many times I hear those words, they still have the same wonderful effect on me. Nothing like the meaningless 'I love yous' that Mark used to mumble whenever he came home drunk—*and guilty.*

I blow her a kiss and then switch off the light. Leaving the door slightly ajar, I make my way towards the stairs. I stop outside Ivy's door. Should I see if she's ready to talk yet? Or maybe eat something?

Best not. She'll only accuse me of being smug and loving every moment of this. I'll leave it until tomorrow.

No—I'm her mother. I shouldn't have to wait. My little girl's in pain, and she needs a shoulder to cry on. Even if she hates me right now, even if she calls me all the names under the sun, I'll still be there for her. It's my job.

"Ivy?" I whisper, tapping on the door. "Can I come in?"

There's no answer.

I check my watch: 10:07 P.M.

Shit, what if she's sleeping? The last thing I want to do is wake her. The poor girl probably hasn't had a decent night's sleep in days.

Putting my ear to the door, I listen out for movement. All I can hear is the faint sound of the TV.

She's awake. I'll check on her. I slowly start to push the door open, bracing myself for a huge shriek, telling me to piss off.

But it doesn't come.

Only the glow of the TV screen lights the room. Ivy is lying on top of the quilt on her side, facing the window. I can't see her face; I can't tell if she's sleeping or crying. *Let her be sleeping. She needs it.*

"Ivy," I whisper. "Are you okay, sweetheart?" She doesn't answer. She's sleeping, thank God.

The TV remote is on the bed next to her. Just as I lean over to scoop it up, I see something on the bed. A dark patch; it surrounds her entire body. *What the hell is that?* Did she spill something? Wine? Don't tell me she's back off the wagon. *She promised me.*

I move closer, kneeling on the bed, and see that it's not red wine.

It's blood.

I frantically switch the light on and race over to her bedside. Heart pounding, unable to catch my breath, I shake her by the shoulders. *This isn't real.* I see the razor blade fall onto the carpet from her dangling arm.

"Ivy!" I sob, staring in dismay at her beautiful face now drained of colour. "Wake up!"

She doesn't respond.

I pick up a shirt from the radiator and quickly wrap it around her sliced wrist.

Thumb to her neck, I feel for a pulse.

There isn't one.

"Wake up, Ivy!" I scream as I part her eyelids. "It's Mummy. *Please!*"

Still nothing.

This isn't happening. Please God, let it be a dream.

Let me wake up.

Climbing onto the bed, I start using CPR on her, the technique somehow coming back to me after all these years.

Open your eyes, sweetheart. Open your eyes.
Breathe!

I start to lose count of how many breaths and chest compressions I've given her.

But nothing has changed. No sound, no movement.

Just stillness.

My throat is closing. My lungs, chest—they're tightening.

I need to get her to the hospital. She needs a doctor.

I race out of the room, my shoulder thudding against the doorframe, and dash into my bedroom. I grab the house phone and call for an ambulance.

But I know my little girl has gone, even before I give the woman my details.

I float across the landing back into Ivy's room, my stomach and heart twisted and torn beyond recognition. None of this feels real.

Because it's not real! It can't be!

I stare down at her for a moment as she sleeps soundly. Her body starts to shrink to Thea's age. No, younger. Much younger. She's five years old and she's passed out on the bed, up late again watching a movie with me in bed. A bowl of popcorn resting on the quilt, a cup of hot chocolate on the bedside cabinet. Why can't these moments last a lifetime? Why does everything have to end? As Ivy's body returns to the present, I pray for time to roll back just a few hours. No—further back. *Much further.* But time has stopped. The space around me is fading fast. An empty void of nothingness.

I climb onto the bed next to her. The quilt is soaked through, but the dampness barely registers. It *is* wine. *It's not my baby's blood. It's not possible.* Draping my arm over her still body, I close my eyes and wait for this nightmare to cease.

I love you, Ivy.

I'm sorry...

3

Ivy is dead.

My mind screams it over and over again, but the words can't physically pass my lips.

Thea is asleep upstairs, all cried out. I'm past crying, too. All I feel is numb, broken—like a speeding train has hit me—and there's nothing left but scattered organs and shattered bones. If it weren't for Thea, getting hit by a train would seem a lot less traumatic.

The living room TV is on, but nothing's sinking in. I know it's some American cop show, but I can't register the plot, who's in it, what the name is. I just don't care. Nothing seems important anymore.

Except Thea.

I went through the first bottle of red in a matter of minutes, and I'm already halfway done with the second. I want to stop—I *need* to stop. Thea's got school in the morning—her first day back. The Head-teacher told her to take as much time as she needed, but Thea actually wants to go. She hasn't seen her friends in weeks, and another day stuck in this house with me would probably be too much. At least school will be a distraction for her. This house is riddled, top to bottom, with reminders of Ivy. Her guitar in the corner of the room, her mass collection of beauty products in the bathroom. And, of course, her bedroom. It's been two months, and I still haven't been able to go in. Mum and Uncle Roy threw out the mattress while I was at the park with Thea. *I couldn't bear the thought of seeing it again.* Every time I pass her door, her room feels like a black hole of pain; one step inside and I'd be whisked off to Hell, to relive that day, over and over again, until I'm reduced to nothing but a shell. Thea will be alone—without a mother—and I will be lost, spiralling into darkness.

All the bedrooms can be locked from the outside with one skeleton key. It's been in the vase on the landing table since we moved in. I never had any reason to use it before. *Well, now I do.* If I could afford to move out, I would—and staying in Mum's isn't an option—no matter how much she begs.

After what happened to Ivy, Mum was the last person I wanted to deal with the mattress. All those memories must have floated back to the surface.

But I suppose it was different with Ivy—she cut her wrists open, bled to death, had every intention of dying. But Mum couldn't be that brave. She tried to take the easy route: an entire bottle of painkillers. Anyone can get drunk and swallow a bunch of pills. It's nothing. It's a piece of cake. Your classic cry for help.

It's when your only daughter has to find you passed out on the bed—that's when things get hard.

But Thea and I *will* be okay. We *will* get through it. Things *will* get better. As long as we have each other.

And as long as Ivy's door stays *locked*.

I take a huge gulp of wine. I wince a little; it's finally started to turn on me. Setting it down on the coffee table, I pick up the remote and switch the TV off. The last place I feel like going is to bed. It's not that I can't sleep—I sleep just fine. It's as if my body just shuts down the moment my head hits the pillow. But sleeping only brings out the nightmares. In the day I can push away those feelings of dread by keeping busy, but when I'm sleeping, there's no escape. And when I wake, for a moment I forget what happened to her, I forget about that *bastard Callum.*

But only for a moment.

I stare at the black screen of the TV, trying to build up the courage to go to bed. *I'm not sleeping on the couch again.* I take a few breaths and finally get up. Normally I'd stumble a little from a bottle and a half of red wine. *Those days have long gone.* Flicking off the light switch, I leave the room, heading for the stairs. In my head, I hear the back door open, and Ivy coming home, staggering across the kitchen, heading for the fridge. Too wasted even to tiptoe. I feel a lump in my throat, cutting through the numbness. I'd give anything to see her face again. *Stoned or not.*

I shake it off and return to a state of detachment. *No good will come of this torture.* I climb the stairs and reach the landing. The first door I pass is the bathroom. Even that whisks me back to that fateful night, watching Thea as she pleaded for her sister to watch a film with her.

What if she'd said yes? Would she still be alive today?

Stop it, Sarah. You're doing it again.

I whiz past Ivy's door, almost holding my breath, and head for Thea's bedroom. Her door is ajar, a blue glow seeping out from its edges. I open it to find the TV on and the sound muted. She's sleeping. I pray her dreams don't torment her like mine do. Let her dream of a future—*a happy one*—even if it's without her sister. I can't see one, though. All I see is a long, dark country road that leads to nowhere.

I pick up Thea's remote and switch the TV off. Her head and arm are dangling out of her bed. I carefully push them back in and readjust her quilt. She looks peaceful, almost content. Maybe sleep is an escape for her. It makes me smile—but only inside. My lips have forgotten how. I stroke her soft hair. For a moment it reminds me of Ivy's.

But only for a moment.

I kiss her on the forehead, whisper that I love her, and then start to leave.

"Ivy?" I hear Thea say, croakily.

"No, sweetheart," I whisper, walking back over to her bedside, "it's Mum."

"I thought you were Ivy," she whispers, staring at me through bloodshot eyes.

"I didn't mean to wake you. I was just turning the TV off."

"I had another dream," she says, quietly. "About Ivy."

I sit on the edge of the bed and gently stroke her hair again. "Did you, sweetheart? What happened?"

"We were playing in the garden."

"That sounds nice," I say with a smile.

Thea shakes her head. "She was being mean to me. Telling me that it was my fault that she died." She bursts into tears. "*It was horrible.*"

I hug her tightly. "Don't cry. It was just a dream. It was no one's fault."

Except mine.

I shush her softly for a few minutes, but it does nothing to settle her.

"Do you want to sleep in my bed tonight?" I ask her. She doesn't answer, but I feel her head nodding against my chest.

I somehow find the strength to pick her up out of bed and carry her to my room. I lay her on my bed, pull the quilt over her, and then climb in next to her. Thea closes her eyes and the crying soon stops. I think she's sleeping. I need to sleep too, but the very notion makes me sick to my stomach. I have to at least try, though. I'm only half a mother when I'm walking around like a zombie, so I close my eyes and wait for sleep to come.

What's another night of torture?

PART II

TEENAGE KICKS

4

I never thought I'd ever say this, but it's great to be finally back at work. Mum thinks it's too soon, but I need the distraction. I suppose I could have switched to mornings instead, but then I'd have no Kate to gossip with. Four years we've worked the night-shift together, and after everything I've been through, she's the only one who can still put a smile on my face. It's a gift. Mum just doesn't get it. She's so busy stuck in that house looking after Dad; she can't see the bigger picture. Bloody hell, the only time she gets to leave that *prick* is to babysit Thea when I'm working.

I'm sitting down on the aisle floor, stacking the lower shelf with tins of tuna. I'm done with crouching; my back can't take it anymore. I see Kate walk up to me, a mischievous grin on her *irritatingly* beautiful face. We don't have a lot in common. She's slim, immaculate teeth, and glowing brunette hair down to the base of her back; tattoos down her right arm, two at the back of her neck, a weed smoker, absolutely *no* kids, and of course she's only twenty-five. And there's me: three stone overweight, crooked teeth, unmanageable brown hair to my shoulders, and too uncool and skint to have a single tattoo. The only thing we have in common is this scruffy little supermarket.

"Check out this guy on the bread aisle," Kate says, prodding me on my shoulder. "He's pissed out of his mind. He's been staring at a package of crumpets for about ten minutes."

Using the shelving for support, I pull myself up, groaning like an elderly woman. I follow her over to the next aisle. I see a balding man, in his early forties, slumped against the shelf staring at the package. "What the hell's he looking for on the label?" I whisper. "They're bloody crumpets, not antibiotics. Should I say something to him?"

"*Nah,*" Kate says with a grin. "Let's just enjoy these little moments when we can. What else is there to amuse us this time of night?"

Tapping her on the arm, I motion with my head

for us to leave him. "We'd better get back to work, otherwise Lenny'll be on our backs again."

"Jesus Christ, Sarah," Kate says, excitement in her tone. "You haven't heard the latest."

We walk back over to the tuna section. "Latest about what?" I ask.

"Lenny won't be barking orders anytime soon. He's been sacked."

"My God," I say, returning to the floor to finish the stacking. "When did this happen?"

"Last Monday night. Police came for him."

"Police? Why?"

"Poisoning."

My eyes widen in shock, unable to comprehend Lenny doing something so vile. "Poisoning? Really?"

Kate leans against the shelf, her face alive with gossip. "Well, apparently his brother was dying of leukaemia."

"Yeah. I remember him mentioning it."

"Well, according to Rebecca, he infected him with vampire blood."

"Oh my bloody God," I say, holding off blurting it out loudly. You don't know who might be listening in this place. "So they've arrested him?"

"Damn right. He's looking at twenty years for that."

I lean against the shelf, shaking my head in astonishment. "That's bonkers. What happened to his brother? I mean—*did he turn?*"

Kate shrugs her shoulders. "I assume so. They took him away somewhere, so it must have worked."

"Well, that's unbelievable. He must have been desperate to risk all that."

"Must have been. Poor bastard."

I glance behind me to make sure a customer isn't eavesdropping. "So what would his brother be like after he turned?"

Kate chuckles. "What am I, a vampire expert?"

"Well, you know more than I do."

Kate shrugs her shoulders. "Well, I suppose he'd get stronger, maybe faster; he wouldn't age as quick; he'd be immune to disease."

I stroke the loose skin under my chin. "A life of slowed-aging? A healthy body? Shit, that doesn't sound all that bad."

Kate chuckles.

"How long would he live?" I ask.

"I don't know. No one knows that for sure. Two, three hundred years maybe?" Kate shakes her head, smiling. "Didn't you pay *any* attention in school?"

"Of course I didn't—otherwise I wouldn't be stuck in this *dump* with you."

Kate playfully punches me in the arm. "Cheeky bitch."

The balding man suddenly appears out of nowhere and grabs a tin of beans from the shelf. I tighten up and grin at him nonchalantly. He returns a grin through rotten teeth, and then wobbles away. "So what did the police do with Lenny's brother?" I ask; this time my voice is much lower.

Kate drags her finger across her throat. "Executed."

"No way would they do that," I say with wide eyes. "It's murder."

A woman pushing a trolley rolls past us. We fall silent for a moment until she's out of sight.

"I'm telling you they do," Kate replies. "They have to. What if Lenny's brother couldn't control his bloodlust? He could have been sucking on your neck this weekend."

"I should be so lucky."

Kate laughs as she carries on pushing tins of tuna onto the shelves. "You're mental, Sarah. You know that?"

"Well, Kate, that *is* some bloody great gossip. Your best yet."

"I aim to please."

"So where did he get the vampire blood from?" I

ask, getting up off the floor. Kate grabs my hands to help. "From the Internet?"

Kate snorts—as if I've just said something ludicrous. "No chance. That stuff online is fake. God knows what they put in it. He must have got it from a real source."

"What, an actual vampire? Lenny?"

"No, of course not. He must have got it from a drug dealer."

My cage of stock is empty, so I push it towards the storeroom to refill it. Kate follows me. "Well," I say, still dazed by the news, "you think you know someone, and then they end up doing something like that."

"I know," Kate replies. "It's madness. Do you think Ivy or Thea would do that for you when you're old and—" Kate's face suddenly drops. "I'm so sorry, Sarah," she says, grabbing my hands, eyes broad with embarrassment. "It just slipped out. I wasn't thinking."

"There's nothing to be sorry about," I reply with a smile. But it's forced because an image of Ivy suddenly pops into my mind. "You can still say her name. She's not Voldemort."

"I know. But it's not just that. You're going

through absolute *hell*, and all I've been doing is talking bullshit all night."

"Don't be silly. Bullshit is exactly what I need right now. All I get at home are reminders of everything that's happened. Mum doesn't help, and Thea? Well, she's dealing with it in her own way. You're the only escape I have left."

"Are you sure?"

I smile. This time it's genuine. "Of course I am, you dick."

"Thanks."

I grab a box and slide it into the cage. "*So*, got any other gossip for me?"

Kate loads up another box. "What? Better than my vampire story?"

"Yeah."

Kate purses her lips, nods, and that mischievous grin returns. "Maybe."

5

"How about another slice of toast?" I ask Thea. It's the third time I've asked, but I can't help myself; she's so skinny these days. She needs a little fattening up.

"No, Mum," Thea protests, waving her hand at me, "I'm full. Stop fussing."

I pour her a glass of juice and set it down on the kitchen table. "Okay, but at least drink something. God knows what rubbish they'll serve in that canteen."

Thea gets up from her chair, rolling her eyes at me. This has become a habit lately. She reminds me of her sister. "The food will be standard food," she replies. "The same when Ivy went there. Nothing's probably changed."

I pick up the glass and present it to her. She rolls

her eyes again, accompanied by a low, pissed-off groan. "*Fine*," she says, reluctantly taking the juice and glugging it down in one.

"See? That wasn't so hard," I say, a pleased smile on my face. "Can't have you getting queasy—especially on your first day."

She unhooks her school bag from the back of the chair and then swings it around her shoulder. "Are you going to be like this every day?"

"Of course not," I reply. *I probably will be.* "I just want everything to go well, that's all. I remember how hard it was for Ivy in that school."

"Look, Mum. You're making it worse. You're putting too much pressure on me."

"I can't help it. It's just tough for me."

"And me," she says, walking over to me. "But it won't be the same. Nothing bad's going to happen. I'm not Ivy. I've got different friends, and I'd never touch drugs—even if you paid me."

I take hold of Thea's soft hands. A lump forms in my throat, a mix of sadness and happiness. A year's a long time in an eleven-year-old's world, but it's nothing in mine. It still feels like yesterday. I think it always will. "Thank you," I say with a smile. "That's good to know. And I'm sorry."

"Don't be. I'll be home at three thirty to tell you all about my day."

I pull Thea in for a hug, squeezing her too hard.

I don't want to let her go.

"You're crushing me," she says, playfully.

"Tough," I reply, fighting hard not to weep. "I'm stuck to you for the day."

I finally release her, kissing her on the cheek. "Be careful today. And stay away from bad crowds. That school is full of them."

"You're doing it again, Mum."

"Sorry, sweetheart," I say, stepping away from her, both hands up in surrender. "I'll see you later for all the gossip."

"Okay." Thea gives me a little wave and then leaves through the back door.

I blow her a kiss, but she doesn't see it. It makes my heart ache. *Don't cry.* Save your tears. She'll be fine. She's strong. She'll be home in no time at all. A new school. A brand new chapter in her life. Nothing bad is going to happen.

She's not Ivy.

6

My second glass of wine doesn't touch the sides. I'm too tense. I've been staring at the back door for the past hour, waiting for Thea to walk through it.

Where the hell is that bloody girl?

She promised she'd be straight home after school. After giving me that lecture, telling me not to worry, and she goes and does something like this.

I glance down at my mobile to see if she's texted me.

She hasn't.

I call her. Voicemail again.

What if something terrible has happened to her?

No, the school would have called.

What if she missed the bus home and had to walk?

No, it's not that far, and she would have called me to come and get her.

Oh my God, what if some paedophile snatched her on the way home?

I'm gonna look for her. Where though? The school? The shopping centre? A friend's house? Christ, I don't even know where half of them live. She could be anywhere.

I take a huge swig of wine, swallow hard, and then grab the bottle for a refill. *Calm down, Sarah.* If I leave now, then she may come home to an empty house. I'll give her a little more time.

That's all you gave Ivy—and look how that turned out.

I fill the glass, spilling a little on the kitchen table. I don't bother wiping it, even though it might stain the wood. It's not important—and it never will be again. I gulp the wine and slam the glass down hard. I can't breathe so I fill it up.

And again, until the bottle is empty.

"Where the hell have you been?" I scream at Thea, too drunk even to get up off the chair.

Thea stares at me as she enters the kitchen, a deep frown across her forehead. "We just decided to get a milkshake on the way home. We weren't that long."

I manage to stand, using the table for support. "Don't *lie* to me!"

"I'm not lying," she replies, backing away from me. "Why would I lie?"

"You've been out with a boy," I snap, pointing my finger like a dagger, struggling to keep my eyes focused on her. "*Haven't you?*"

"Mum, it's only just gone five."

"You promised me that you'd be home by half past three." I start to stagger towards her. "You let me sit here, worried *sick*, for almost two hours."

Thea slips past me, heading towards the hallway. "No one asked you to do that."

"Don't speak to me like that!" I shout, following her out of the kitchen. "You're going to end up *dead* —just like your sister."

She doesn't retort as she disappears upstairs.

"Is that what you want?" I yell up from the foot of the stairs. "Do you want to end up lying *dead* in a pool of blood? *Do you?* You don't know what I've been through! You think you've had it hard—well you don't know the meaning of the word!"

"Shut up, Mum!" Thea weeps from the landing. "Just leave me alone."

I hear the sound of her bedroom door slamming shut. I think about going up to her, telling her that she's grounded, that tomorrow I'll be picking her up from school. But instead, I sit, slouched on the first step, staring at the hallway floor.

My head drops into my hands and I start to sob.

PART III

FAMILY BLOOD

7

Eighteen Months Later...

Kate stares at me like I've got a piece of food in my teeth. "I'm fine," I tell her. "Stop looking at me."

"You're not fine," she replies, picking up two loaves of bread from the cage. "You've been like a bloody zombie all shift. What's wrong with you?"

I want to tell her about the week I've had, but I just don't have the energy. Eventually, she'll get it out of me; she has a gift. But right now, all I want to do is get through this night shift and sleep off a pounding headache.

"Look, Sarah," Kate continues, "I know you're probably sick of talking about your problems—but without listening to you *drone on* about your horrible life, I've got nothing to entertain me. And you wouldn't want to see me unentertained. I can get up to *all* sorts of mischief."

I smile, unable to hold it off. I was right: this woman truly *is* gifted. "Okay, you win. As usual." I sit down on a stack of empty bread crates. "It's Thea again."

"What about her?"

I shrug my shoulders. "Exactly. I'm starting to think I don't know a single thing about her. She's always on that computer of hers chatting to God knows who, and then when I ask her anything about school, she just grunts and says everything's great. It's like she's turned into a different person."

Kate chuckles. "I may not have any children, but you just described practically every thirteen-year-old in the world."

"Yeah, I know what you're saying, but you haven't seen the way she looks at me."

"What do you mean?"

"Well, for instance, last week, she came home late from a friend's house—*again*—and I asked her why she didn't phone me, and she just looked at me like I was a piece of rubbish." I peer down at the floor, shaking my head. "I think she hates me."

Kate walks over to me, placing her hand on my

arm. "Don't be silly, Sarah—she loves you. She's just young; that's all. She's probably testing out her boundaries. I used to do the same with my mother. Didn't you?"

"I suppose," I reply, shrugging exactly like Thea does when I'm pointing out something obvious to her.

"*See?* And you're so lucky. I'd give anything to have what you have."

I snort. "What, a fat ass and a huge mortgage?"

"No," she replies. "A real family. I'd love to have a daughter to bitch about."

"Really? I didn't think you were bothered."

"Hey, just because I enjoy the occasional joint, doesn't mean that I don't think about having kids someday. I'm not getting any younger, Sarah. The clock is ticking."

"Well, I don't think you'd be quite so keen if you bumped into Thea right now."

"Look, stop sulking moany-bones and help me with this box."

Normally I'd gladly help her, but tonight all I feel like doing is sitting here and doing bugger all.

Kate takes out the last loaf of bread, and then looks over at me, grimacing. "Come on—don't just sit there watching."

"Not tonight, Kate. I just haven't got it in me. I think I'm going to ask Darren if I can go home early."

"Really?" she asks, eyes wide with shock. "That's a first."

I nod my head, and then come off the crate. "Yeah. I'm going to tell him I've got a headache."

"Are you sure? He'll dock your pay."

"I don't care if he does."

"What's the point of going home? Thea is safe, tucked up in bed. Your mother's more than capable of watching her."

"It's not just that. Mum isn't in the best shape to be babysitting tonight, especially if Thea starts playing up again."

"How come?"

"Dad's cancer's come back. It's not looking good."

"Oh God, I'm so sorry," Kate says, eyes wide with sympathy. "I didn't realise. Is there anything I can do? Maybe I can sit with Thea one night. Give you and your mother a break."

"No, it's fine. I'm just going to get back to the house."

Kate gives me a hug. This is exactly what I need, but I don't show any emotion on my face—I'm too drained. "Thanks, Kate," I say, pulling out of it. "I'll see you next week."

"Okay," Kate replies, rubbing the side of my arm. "Call me if you need anything."

"Will do."

The store is busier than usual; I bet Darren will kick up a fuss that I'm leaving. Maybe I should tell him about Dad. No, he'll ask too many questions, and I'm just not in the mood. I just need to talk to him and get the hell out this place.

Even before I've opened the front door, I can hear Mum's voice. She's shouting.

My fingers scramble into my handbag and I dig out the house keys in record time. In a panic, I open the door and burst into the hallway. Mum is standing at the top of the stairs. I can't see Thea.

"What's all the shouting about?" I ask as I make my way up to the landing. At the top I see Thea standing by her bedroom door, her face burning red with rage, iPad under her arm.

"This little madam just won't listen to me," Mum says; memories of my mischievous childhood flooding back. "I've told her it's too late to talk to her friends on the computer—but she's not having any of it."

"It's only ten o clock!" Thea screams, tears running down her cheeks. "This is the only time we get to talk."

"It's a school night," Mum points out. "You can talk to them tomorrow."

"Tell her, Mum," Thea orders me. "Tell her that it's not late. I'm thirteen!"

My head starts to pound even more, temples throbbing. This is the last thing I need right now. "Look, Thea, Gran's right. It's way past your bedtime, so hand over the tablet."

"That's not fair!" Thea cries. "You always let me use it!"

"Not at this time of night," I reply. "I had no idea you stayed up so late to talk to your friends."

"That's because you're always too drunk to notice!" she snaps.

My mouth drops when I hear her poisonous words. How dare she say something so vicious! Like I'm nothing more than some drunken idiot. I'm her mother, for Christ's sake!

"That's just not true," I retort, wishing that I'd just stayed in work. "A couple of glasses of wine does *not* make me an alcoholic."

Mum shakes her head and starts to make her way downstairs, brushing past me, her stomping feet echoing across the landing. "She's your problem now. You deal with her. I need to sit down."

Once Mum has disappeared into the living room, I walk towards Thea, rubbing my aching head, trying to will the pain away. "Look, sweetheart," I say, as softly as I can, "you should be in bed. It's late. If it were the weekend then it'd be different. But it's not, so hand it over."

Thea glares at me; that vicious look she gave me when I said she couldn't sleep over Ellie's house. *"Fine then—have it,"* she says, spitting her words at me as she hands me the device. If it didn't cost the earth, I think she would have happily thrown it at me.

"Thank you," I say. "It's for your own good."

"What would you know about what's good for me?"

"What's that supposed to mean?" I ask.

"All you do is shout," she says. "You never bother to talk to me."

"I try to talk to you all the time, but you never give me a straight answer. You go out; you don't tell me where you're going. You come home late from school; I don't even get a bloody text. So I'm just left in the kitchen, staring at that back door, thinking something terrible has happened."

"I *do* tell you."

I grunt. "Yeah, when you feel like it. I worry about you all the time, Thea. I'm petrified that you'll end up like your sister."

"I'm *nothing* like Ivy. When are you going to understand? She was a selfish sister—*and a fucking junkie!*"

I slap Thea across the face.

Time freezes for a moment, but then unfreezes when she bursts into tears and slams the door in my face.

My hand shakes as I bring it up to my mouth. *Did I really just hit my daughter in the face? No, I couldn't have. I don't hit. I'm not Dad. I'd never lay a finger on my family.*

Never!

Thea's sobbing bleeds onto the landing. The sound makes my body tighten. I knock the door gently but she screams for me to go away. I think about opening the door anyway, but I just leave her there, crying. I see an image of Ivy, coming home from school, sobbing until her entire face is swollen —too afraid to tell me about the baby, but too huge a

48

burden to carry alone. The memory cuts through me and my throat catches.

I feel sick; my headache is getting worse. I make my way downstairs, hands still trembling. I can feel my mind trying to repress the memory of hitting Thea. But that never works.

Mum is in the living room, so I slip past the door and enter the kitchen. I open the cupboard and pull out a bottle of red. Filling a glass up, I sit at the table, staring at the back door.

I *definitely* should have stayed in work.

8

I'm sitting in Mum's living-room armchair, staring at a dying man. This is the last place I want to spend my Saturday afternoon. But I'm here to support Mum. She's been through hell these last few years, and now it looks like Dad's time is almost up. I've tried to feel pity for him, for the pain he's going through—but it's not as easy as it sounds. The only person who'll miss him is Mum, and I'm terrified that once he's gone, she'll start to lose interest in living. Before he got sick, she needed his addiction to give her life purpose. She's a problem solver; and Dad getting lung cancer was just another one to fix. But now that's over. He'll be dead in months, and there are no *maybes* this time. Once the chemo has stopped, that's it. No more Dad.

I *will* cry at the funeral; I'm certain of it—but not for him. Only for Mum, and, of course, Uncle Roy.

Dad has insisted that he dies at home. I don't blame him; the last place I'd want to see out my days is a stuffy old hospital. *No, thank you.*

He's been fast asleep on the couch since Thea and I arrived, wheezing loudly with every strained breath. Mum says I should forgive and forget before it's too late. But I already have. At least *forgiven*. Forgetting is a bit of a stretch. She thinks that I won't mourn him because I'm angry, that I wish him dead. But that's not true. I wouldn't wish anyone dead. I just don't feel anything for him. After years of watching him coming home blind drunk, or swinging punches at Mum, or vomiting over the carpet, all he is to me is a stranger. And it's bloody hard to mourn a stranger.

Thea is sitting on the armchair, watching *Toy Story 2* on the TV. She barely knows her grandfather. She only started seeing him after the diagnosis, and before that he was just an old drunk that I kept the girls away from.

Thea and I haven't talked to each other since Wednesday. I've tried to engage, but all I get in return are teenage-grunts. And 'sorry' has done absolutely nothing to soften what I did to her.

After the way she spoke to Mum about that iPad, I was planning on grounding her. But then I hit her, and punishing her suddenly didn't seem all that fair.

I still can't believe I did it. It's just not in my nature. Am I turning into Dad? Has he managed to get his claws into me after all these years?

No! Never!

I'm nothing like that asshole!

Mum doesn't know that I hit Thea, and I think I'll keep it that way. It's so mortifying, and she has enough on her plate already without worrying about my dramas.

"You hungry, Thea?" Mum asks as she pokes her head into the living room. She always cooks when she's stressed; the kitchen is a safe haven for her. Dad always stayed in the living room, curled up on the couch, either shouting at the TV or passed out. A fitting place to die really.

"No thank you, Gran," Thea replies, shaking her head, her eyes locked on the screen, "I'm fine."

"Are you sure? It's pizza. The ones you like."

Thea turns to her grandmother. "Honestly, I'm fine. I had a late breakfast."

That's a lie. I let it slide, though. Now's not the time for another row about skipping meals.

"Okay, love," Mum replies, turning to me. "How about you then, Sarah? You want some pizza?"

I'm not hungry but I think Mum could use the distraction, so I say, "Yes, please. But not too much. I'm trying to cut down a bit. Summer's coming."

Mum tuts, and then disappears into the kitchen. I follow her in. I could use a break from Thea's steel wall of silence. Mum is staring into an open oven; there're puffs of steam coming out. "Nearly ready," she says with confidence, closing the door. With her back to me, she swills something at the sink. Leaning against the worktop, I wait for her to finish. When she doesn't turn for over a minute, I walk up to her. Mum is running cold water over the same plate. "Are you okay?" I ask, placing my hand on the side of her arm.

She doesn't answer.

I hear a snivel; she's crying. Reaching over her, I turn the tap off. "Mum?"

Sniffing loudly, she turns to me, wipes the tears from her eyes and smiles. It looks forced. "I'm fine, Sarah. Honestly."

"You don't *seem* fine."

"It's nothing. I'm just having a funny five minutes, that's all. It's been a tough few days."

To see her like this pains me, no matter how I

feel about Dad. "Come here," I say, pulling her in for a hug, trying to hide the sadness in my voice.

Mum starts to cry into my shoulder as I stroke her back. Even when Dad was at his most violent, I'd never see her break. She's always been so tough, like nothing on earth could faze her.

"I can't lose him, " she sobs. "I just want him to be healthy again."

As far as I'm concerned, that man has *never* been healthy. "I'm sorry, Mum, but he's in so much pain—it's better this way."

She pulls out of the hug, a deep scowl across her brow. "You'd rather he was dead—*wouldn't you? You'd rather he was just wiped off the face of the earth? Just admit it, Sarah.*"

"Don't say things like that. I wouldn't wish anyone dead. Just because Dad and I don't see eye to eye, doesn't mean that I want you to lose him."

Mum shakes her head. "Well, I won't be losing him. Not on my watch, anyway."

"What are you talking about? The chemo's over."

"He doesn't need chemo," Mum replies. "I'll take matters into my own hands—not some useless doctor who doesn't give a shit about him."

"What are you talking about?" I ask, frowning with confusion. *Mum's finally lost it.*

She doesn't answer.

"Mum?"

"Look, just trust me, will you?" she finally replies. "I'm going to help your father, so let's just leave it at that."

What the hell is she talking about? "You can't just *leave it at that*. Tell me."

"I don't want to tell you because you'll say that it's stupid."

"No I won't." *There's a good chance I will.*

Mum lets out long exhale. "*Fine*—if you must know, I'm going to give your father vampire blood."

"What!" I can't help but laugh out loud. *Vampire blood?* Did she really just say that? "Tell me you're joking?"

"*See?*" she says, shaking her head, clearly annoyed with me. "That's why I didn't want to tell you."

"So this isn't a wind up then? You're serious."

"Of course I'm serious! Your father is dying in there, Sarah, so the last thing I'd do is joke about it."

"Yes, but, Mum—vampire blood? *Really?*"

"Look, I know it'll be expensive, but it'd be worth every penny. One dose and he'll be his old self again. *Better even.* He won't age; he won't get sick. It can be like it was before."

"What are you talking about, Mum? He was an asshole! Have you forgotten what he did to us? All those nights spent at Auntie Julie's house when he was on the warpath. Has all that *slipped your mind?*"

"For God's sake, Sarah! That was years ago! Your father's a changed man. You haven't noticed because you and Thea never bother coming 'round."

I chuckle; bewildered that she could be so deluded. "And why the hell is that?"

"Because you're spiteful. You never give anyone a second chance. It's Sarah's way—or it's *no way!*"

I shake my head, my body tightening; flashes of Dad flood my mind. I see him pulling Mum's hair until she's on all fours like a dog; I see him chasing me around the garden, threatening to burn all my toys. How dare she says these things! "Well, if I'm stubborn," I retort, "then I wonder where I got it from!"

I watch her lips try to form a fitting response, but nothing comes out. So the kitchen becomes silent instead.

It's painful.

I feel like grabbing Thea and leaving right this second, away from this crazy woman. Away from that *wanker* in the living room. But then Mum breaks out into tears, and I crumble, put my resentment to one side, and pull her into a second hug.

"*I'm sorry, Sarah,*" Mum weeps, her words almost muted. "*I didn't mean what I said. You're a good person.*"

I shush her gently. "It's okay. I know you didn't mean it. I'm here for you—no matter what."

Mum moves her head away from my shoulder and then looks at me, her eyes streaming, bloodshot. "Then you'll get it for me?"

"Get what?"

"The blood."

She can't be serious. "Are you crazy?" I ask, stepping away from her. "You can't turn him into a vampire."

Mum wipes the tears away with her sleeve. "Why not?"

"For one thing, it's illegal. If the police found out, you're looking at twenty years in prison. And then Dad would be taken away and killed by the government."

"You don't think I know all that? *Of course I do.* But what the hell have I got to lose? Living with this cancer has been worse than any prison sentence. Your father will be *dead* in a few months, maybe even sooner. But at least this gives him a chance."

"You've lost your mind! You're talking about

turning Dad into a bloody vampire! What happens afterwards? What if he attacks you? Yeah, he might get his health back, but he'll be a lot stronger than he was. What if he's more aggressive, too?"

"Then I'll cross that bridge when I come to it. But right now, all I've got to look forward to is a life without your father. And that's not something I'm ready for."

"Look, Mum, I love you, and the last thing I want is to see you unhappy, but if you want to risk your life, or jail, then you're on your own. I want absolutely no part in it whatsoever."

"*Fine*. I can get it myself. You can get it on the Internet anyway."

"No, you can't," I say, shaking my head. "That stuff is fake."

"Then I'll get it from somewhere else."

This is madness! I feel like I've just stepped into *The Twilight Zone*. I clench my fists in anger, and then slam one down on the worktop. "Just stop it, Mum! You can't do this! You're going to get yourself hurt, and I don't need this shit right now. I've already lost one daughter, and I don't want to lose you as well. So enough of this *bullshit!*"

"The pizza's burning," Thea says from the kitchen doorway, pointing over at the smoking oven.

I race over to it and open the door. I grab the oven glove and pull out the baking tray with the black pizza on top. Placing it down by the sink, I notice that Mum is swilling that plate again, clearly concealing her tears from Thea.

"What's all the shouting about?" Thea asks. "You woke up Granddad."

Mum sniffs loudly and then races past Thea, disappearing out of the kitchen.

"Is she all right?" Thea continues. "I think she was crying."

I lean against the worktop, feeling drained and shell-shocked. "She's fine, Thea. She's just upset about Granddad, that's all. We both are." It suddenly dawns on me that this is the most Thea's said to me since Wednesday night.

"Oh, right. Okay," she says as if it's no big deal. But she's only thirteen, and she's already lost a sister. Losing a grandfather she barely knows is hardly big news. "Can we go now?"

I grin at her, thinking that that's the smartest thing anyone has said all day. "Of course we can." Should I ask her if we're cool? No, I better not; I'll only end up blowing it.

Thea goes out into the hallway to get her jacket from the banister. I pop my head into the living room and see Mum sitting next to Dad. His eyes are shut. At least he's sleeping again. She's stroking his legs as they lie across her lap, her eyes still filled with tears. "Mum?" I whisper. "Are you going to be okay?"

She nods, with a slight smile as if to say: *I'm better now.*

"Thea and I are heading off," I say. "Do you need anything before we go?"

"No. You get off home now," she replies, her tone snarky as she turns away from me, her eyes on Dad as he stirs beside her (no different after fifteen pints of cider). "Don't worry about *us*—we'll be just fine."

The guilt-trip usually works on me. But this isn't a request to pick up some shopping from the town, or take her car to be valeted. We could both get into trouble.

So this time, she's on her own.

And this time, I mean it too. I've got my own problems to deal with.

"Okay then," I reply, firmly. "I'll see you in a few days."

She doesn't respond.

"*Fine,*" I say under my breath, making my way out.

As I reach the front door, I stop in my tracks. *She*

wasn't serious. Was she? No, she's just hurting. It's just the stress talking. She'd never be that irresponsible.

I leave Mum's house and meet Thea by the car. She half-smiles at me when I open the door for her.

A half-smile? That's progress. A bar of chocolate and I'm golden.

9

———

Thea is late for school for the second time this week. If she wasn't so busy on that phone of hers she might be a little more organised.

"It's almost eight," I remind her. "You're going to miss your bus again."

Thea ignores my comment, continuing to speed-text someone. *Who is it this time? Ellie? Beth? Faith maybe?*

A boy?

No, she would've mentioned it to me.

Like hell, she would!

"Put your phone down," I say, "or I'm flushing it down the toilet."

"*God, Mum*," Thea replies, bitterly; eyes still locked on the screen, "will you get off my case."

"If you miss that bus you can walk to school this time. I'm not bloody driving you."

Chuckling, she finally looks up at me. "Yeah right. With all the lectures about safety, and you're gonna make me walk on my own, among all the paedos and rapists?"

"Don't get smart with me."

Thea tuts loudly and gets up from the chair, leaving the phone on the table. "Fine. You win. I'm going." She then makes her way out onto the hallway.

"Where are you going now? Your bag is in here."

"I'm getting my coat," I hear her voice shout down from the landing. "Is that *okay with you*?"

I'll be glad when she's gone for the day. Need to sleep off this hangover. Shouldn't have had that wine last night.

Just as I'm about to take a sip of my orange juice, I notice Thea's phone. It's unattended. That's a rare sight. Before I even have a moment to ponder the morals of snooping through Thea's possessions, I'm grasping the phone in my left hand, reading her last few texts.

Who the fuck is Jared?

I scroll down to read a few more.

A boyfriend?

"That's mine!" Thea says from the kitchen doorway. My heart jolts a little, nearly dropping the phone.

Flustered, I hand it over to her, and she snatches it from me. "Are you seeing someone?" I ask her.

Thea slips her jacket on, grabbing her school bag from the back of the chair, her face bright red with anger. "That's got nothing to do with you. Those were *private* messages."

"How old is this boy?"

"It's none of your business!"

"Of course it's my business!" I snap. "I'm your *mother* for Christ's sake!"

"That doesn't give you the right to go through my things. Did you do that with Ivy, too? Is that why she left with Callum?"

My stomach twists when I hear Ivy's name. "No. Your sister left with that *junkie* because I *didn't* go through her things. Keeping out of her life is what got her killed. So shoot me if I'm not prepared to make the same mistake again."

Thea doesn't answer; she just looks at me with Ivy's venomous eyes. She slips the phone into her pocket, shakes her head, and then heads for the back door.

"You stay away from that boy!" I warn her as she disappears outside. "I mean it! Or I'll be down that school so—"

The door slams hard, cutting me off mid-rant. I think about chasing after her. Instead I'm left staring at the back door.

Just another day in the life of Sarah Wilkes.

Mum lets herself into the kitchen through the back door. Normally I hate going into work, but after this morning's row with Thea, I'll gladly take the distraction.

"How are you holding up, Mum?" I ask her as she takes off her jacket.

"Don't worry about me," she replies with a tone. "Your father's the one who's dying."

Out of view, I roll my eyes and put the remark to one side. I can do without her on my back as well. "Sorry," I say, swallowing my pride like sandpaper. "How's Dad doing?"

Mum turns to me with a pitiful look. Lately, Mum's eyes have been permanently bloodshot. "The doctor says that he should be in a hospice."

"Maybe they're right. It can't be good for him stuck on the couch all day."

"That's where he wants to be. He hates being upstairs on his own, and he doesn't want to die in some bloody hospice."

Slipping my cardigan on, I hear Thea stomping around in her bedroom, clearly making more noise than usual. Is she trying to annoy me? If she is, then it's working. "Look, Mum, maybe you should stay at home. I'm sure my boss can find someone to cover the night shift."

Mum shakes her head, walks over to the kettle, and flicks the switch. "No, it's fine. Uncle Roy is down for a few days. They said they'd call if there's an emergency. And besides, I love spending time with Thea, even if it is only an hour or two before she goes to bed."

I grab my handbag from the table and hook it over my shoulder. "Well, you've got your work cut out. She's not talking to me again."

Taking out a mug from the cupboard, she sets it down on the worktop. "Oh, what's happened now?" she asks, in a voice that suggests that whatever the problem is, I'm either overreacting, or that it would *never* happen on her watch.

"Thea's got a boyfriend, and she's angry with me for checking her phone messages."

The kettle finishes boiling, and Mum pours herself a coffee. "You checked her phone? Well, what did you think would happen?"

I don't bother retorting; there's no point. I open the kitchen door and poke my head into the hallway. "Thea!" I shout up to her. "Gran's here, so I'm off to work. I'll see you in the morning."

I wait for a response, but all I hear is more stomping around. That's the best I'm going to get out of her this evening. Sighing, I scoop up my car keys from the table and head for the back door. "Okay, I'll see you tomorrow, Mum. Text me if you have any problems, or news about Dad."

Stirring her coffee, she starts to well up again. "Okay, Sarah." She turns away from me to face the worktop. "Have a good shift," she struggles to say.

I feel like I'm stuck in limbo: one foot in the kitchen, and the other outside. Should I call in sick? Surely they'd understand what with Dad the way he is. They don't know how I feel about him. In fact, I don't have to mention Dad. Mum's well-being is enough to warrant some work leave.

The sound of Mum's spoon hitting the inside of the mug increases.

I don't know what to do?

But then a voice in my head tells me to go and leave her in peace. So I listen and I'm out the door, heading for the car.

Roll on ten-hour shift.

10

I'm a half hour early for work. The break-room is empty so I make myself a coffee and pull out my phone. I haven't been able to get Mum's request out of my head. Was it such an unreasonable thing to ask? The man is dying. What other way *is there* to save him?

I wish I'd paid more attention in school instead of daydreaming and chatting with Mark. Vampires *always* came up in history class. *Every bloody term.* I could have been an expert by now.

I take a sip of coffee and start to surf the net, reading various articles and forums about vampire infection. Finally, I settle on my usual haunt for facts: Wikipedia. It claims that the speed someone turns all depends on the host. For some, the changes can start within a few hours. While for others, it could take days, even weeks. Strength and bone density improves; so does immunity to disease and healing capabilities, which slows the ageing process dramatically. But these changes also cause vampire skin to be highly sensitive to sunlight, causing hibernation during the day. Oddly enough, scaling walls like spiders and enslaving their hosts using psychic powers didn't come up at all. *What a surprise!*

The blood cravings are apparently like any addiction: they can be controlled over time and with restraint. Some are worse than others, but all a vampire needs to survive is around two or three hundred millilitres of blood per day. It can be from human or animal, but always warm. Once the cravings are under control, vampires can quite easily blend in among ordinary people, making them almost impossible to spot.

They make it sound so easy, but it won't be—especially for an ex-alcoholic. Can someone like Dad really control himself?

Putting the phone on the table, I sigh loudly; frustrated that Mum has even put this notion into my head.

I take a sip of coffee, lean back on my chair, and then close my eyes. *Bloody vampires.*

"Where might someone get hold of vampire blood?" I ask Kate without double-checking that the break-room is deserted. *Stupid*, but I've got a lot on my mind at the moment.

Kate nearly chokes on her grape juice, her eyes wide with shock. "Why the hell would you ask me something like that?"

"Oh, it doesn't matter," I reply, taking a sip of tea. Maybe she thinks it was just a dumb joke. "I was just curious."

Kate shakes her head, clearly seeing through my bullshit. "Sarah, I've known you for a long time now, so I know when you're hiding something. So go on—spit it out. Why would you want vampire blood?"

I brace before answering. "It's my mother. She said she wanted to infect my father with it."

"Really? Carol? Bloody hell," Kate says, shaking her head in disbelief. "And I thought *my* parents were nuts."

"I think she's finally lost it. She asked me if I could get it for her. I told her no."

"*Shit*. Does she even know what'll happen to her if she gets caught?" Kate asks, taking another sip of her juice.

"Yeah. She knows everything. But even when the bastard's dying, he's still got a hold over her. She told me that it's worth the risk."

"So do you think she'd go through with it?" Kate asks. "Or is it just the grief talking?"

"No, I think she's very serious," I reply with a confident nod. "She's always serious when it comes to him. She's capable of anything."

"What do you mean?"

I pause for a moment, wondering whether or not I should tell her the truth about Mum. Trust has never been an issue with Kate—but family shame, that's a very different beast.

"You don't have to tell me if you don't want to," Kate continues, clearly sensing my reluctance. "I'll mind my own business. It'll be hard, but I think I can make an exception for you."

"It's fine," I reply. "I don't mind telling you. But keep it to yourself though."

"Of course," she replies. "You can trust me. Mum's the word."

Poor choice of words.

"Before my father got sick, he was a nasty piece of work. He was an alcoholic. He used to beat my mother and me. *Christ*, he wasn't that nice sober."

"Oh, that's awful, Sarah. I'm so sorry. I had no idea."

"It's fine. Not a lot of people know. Ivy knew, and Thea sort of knows, but I don't tell her *all* the grizzly details. That's why I've kept the girls away from him. I mean, he got clean before he got cancer, but I could never forgive him for what he put us through. I remember I was around Thea's age, and he came home pissed up as usual, ranting about losing all his pay at the dog tracks. A sure thing according to that man—the same as every tip he had. I don't even recall what triggered him to take his belt off and hit me with it. The prick had no problem using his fists, but he'd never used a belt before. So there I was, screaming for him to stop. Begging for him just to let me go to bed. I can still feel those massive welts throbbing in my mind. After about ten lashes, the bastard suddenly stopped dead. I remember thinking that he'd come to his senses, seen the error of his ways. But then his eyes closed and his body went limp. It was so weird. And there was Mum, standing behind him, grasping the poker with both hands."

"Oh my God. That's terrible," Kate says. "So what happened to your father?"

"Sadly, very little. He had a concussion and a few

stitches. But Mum wasn't so lucky. Later that night she went up to bed and took an overdose of painkillers. Ended up in the hospital *with him*."

Kate's jaw is hanging wide open in horror. I half wish I hadn't let the cat out of the bag. But it's too late now. Unfortunately, I don't feel any better for sharing it. "That's when he stopped drinking," I continue. "After that, he went to AA, and Mum has spent the last twenty odd years keeping him healthy."

"Now I see what you mean with the vampire blood."

"Exactly. She'll do anything for him."

Kate finishes the rest of her drink. "Do you think she'll do something stupid when your father dies?"

"Yes."

Kate gets up off her chair and heads over to the washbasin. "If you're that worried," she says, sitting back down, "then I might know someone who can get some."

"Really? What, genuine vampire blood?"

"Keep your voice down," Kate whispers, eyes racing to the slightly ajar break-room door. "You wanna get us thrown in jail?"

I mouth a *sorry* and then lean over the table, my head low. "How much would it cost?"

"I don't know," she replies, shrugging her shoulders. "I'm guessing it's expensive. You're probably looking around five grand. Maybe more."

"So who the hell do you get it from?" I ask, keeping my voice down. "A real vampire?"

Kate chuckles. "No, of course not. The guy I get my weed from can get pretty much anything for the right price."

"How will I know if it's fake or not?"

Kate purses her lips. "I don't know, Sarah. This isn't exactly my field of expertise. Remember, I'm not a hundred percent he can even get it; all I can do is ask."

"Mum's got the money. I know she'd pay anything."

"Yeah, I bet. But I don't want to go to him unless you're positive you want the stuff—because the dealer's a right nasty prick."

I lean back in my chair, letting out a lungful of stressed-out air. I still think that Mum is crazy, but she's bound to give up if she loses Dad. And I can't *bear* losing anyone else.

"I want some," I tell her, with a sudden burst of confidence. "Definitely."

Kate shakes her head again. "I think you're bloody bonkers, Sarah. But I'll do it for you."

"Thank you."

What the hell am I doing? I think Mum and Thea have finally sent me over the edge.

I take another sip of tea. "Do you think it's true what they say—you know, about vampire slaves?"

Kate laughs. "What are you talking about?"

"That if you drink the blood then the vampire can find you wherever you are. And then you belong to them for life."

"Yes, it's true," she replies with a spooky voice and straight face—but I can see the smirk bursting to get out. "Vampires have *psychic powers*, and they also have *no reflection in the mirror*."

"Piss off," I say with a grin.

Sniggering, Kate gets off the chair, heading for the toilet. "And they can turn into *bats as well*."

11

I've been sitting on my bed, staring at the blood for the last thirty minutes. Why the hell did I let Mum guilt-trip me? I thought I was stronger than that. And I should have never got Kate involved. Even possession carries a ten-year sentence—and here it is, in my hand, a small vial. Blood from an actual vampire. For some reason, I imagined that it would look different. I mean, I expected it to be blood, but, well—just different. Christ, it could well be human blood. Even sheep's blood for all I know.

Or red wine. I take a sip of mine, finishing off the glass, and then sigh, realising that I've made a terrible mistake. What the hell was I thinking? I should flush the blood down the toilet, and put this ordeal behind me. Mum doesn't even know that I have it yet. I could easily say that the deal fell through. But then she'd want her five grand back, and I definitely don't have that kind of money lying around.

To hell with it! It's only money. I can owe it. I can't possibly give this to her. What if he turns into something even more *hideous* than before?

I unscrew the cap at the top of the vial and sniff the blood. It doesn't smell of anything.

Shit, what if smelling it infects me?

Calm down, it's blood, not cocaine. I screw the lid back on quickly.

And what if she can't get enough animal blood to feed him? What then? He could turn on her. On the postman. The neighbours. *Jesus, bloody Christ, this is insane. I'm not doing it. The old bastard can die as far as I'm concerned.*

Thea and I will have to watch Mum like a hawk, day and night. She'll soon get over him. Husbands die every day. She's not the first woman to lose someone close. I lost my little girl; she was innocent. Dad is most definitely *not*. Mum will just have to cope with it, and that's that.

I see a horrid image of Mum, lying on her bed; her wrist sliced, the mattress soaked through in blood. The sight goes through me, and I shudder.

The sound of the back door opening and slamming shut travels up to my bedroom. *Thea's home from school.* In a panic, I quickly leap off the bed and stuff the vial into my sock drawer. I take a few breaths to settle my nerves and then leave the room. I glance down at my watch: it's almost half three. She's home on time. Miracles *can* happen.

Thea comes trudging up the stairs towards me.

"Where's the fire?" I ask her as she passes me on the landing.

"I need my iPad," she replies, disappearing into her bedroom.

"What's the big rush?" I ask, walking over to her doorway. Her bedroom is in such a state; it's no wonder she can't find anything.

"Some friends are picking me up," she replies as she searches her bed and desk. "We're going into town."

"What friends?"

"Some friends from school. No one you know."

I can feel my blood start to boil as I watch her fling pieces of clothing onto the floor. "Is Jared going to be there?"

"Maybe. So what if he is? We're just friends."

I want to shake her, tell her that teenage boys are only interested in one thing, but that will only end up making matters worse. "Listen to me, Thea. I'm not comfortable with you going out on a school night to see some boy."

Thea finds the tablet underneath the pillow and then glares at me. "He's not some *boy*. He's a good friend. And you can't tell me who I can and can't hang out with."

"Yes, I bloody can if I think you might get hurt."

Thea snorts. "That's ridiculous. You don't know the first thing about Jared. He could be a Saint for all you know."

"Well that's exactly why I don't want you seeing him. For all I know, he could be another Callum."

"Callum?" Thea laughs out loud. Does she think this is some kind of joke? Well I'm not laughing. "Jared is nothing like that loser. You keep comparing my life with Ivy's as if I want to end up like her. Screw you, Mum. I lost a sister too. Do you really think I'm going to start taking drugs, get an abortion and wind up killing myself? Do you?"

I can feel my chin start to quiver. I fight it off. There's no room for tears when it comes to Thea. "Don't you dare speak to me like that! This has nothing to do with your sister. This is *me* being a good parent."

"Ha! A good parent? That's rich coming from an alcoholic."

I try to slap Thea across the face, but she catches my wrist.

"See what I mean," she continues. "You call yourself a good parent? I would *never* hit someone across the face. I didn't learn that from you. I learned it from being a decent human being."

I think about hitting her with my other hand, but then I see Dad hitting Mum, and I come to my senses. *I'm not my father!* Pulling out of her grip, I take a step back. "I didn't mean to," I say, trying to calm my trembling hands. "I'm sorry."

Thea shakes her head, disgust in her eyes. "So you should be." Brushing past me, she marches towards the landing. "I'll see you later. When you've sobered up."

"No you won't," I tell her as she reaches the top of the stairs. "You'll see me now."

She stops in her tracks, turning to me with a giant grimace. "What are you talking about?"

"You're grounded. You're not setting *foot* out of that front door."

"What! You can't stop me."

"Yes, I bloody can. I'm your mother."

"So? I'm your daughter. I'm allowed to have a life, you know."

"Yeah, but while you're under *my* roof, you'll

obey *my* rules. And I say you're grounded for a week."

Thea's face turns red instantly. I can see her grip on the banister tighten. She hates me; I know she does. But if I don't do this now, if I don't take a stand, then in another year she'll end up just like Ivy. And that ain't happening!

"You can't do that!" Thea screams. "It's not fair!"

"Yes, it bloody *is* fair, madam. And don't even think about sneaking out because so help me God, I'll smash that iPad to bits. And your pocket money; that'll go too. Are we clear?"

For the first time in years, Thea is lost for words. Have I cracked it? Is a firm hand all it takes? A few more ground rules?

Is that why I lost Ivy?

Thea storms past me, back into her bedroom. "I hate you!" she screeches as she slams the door behind her. "I never want to speak to you again!"

I think about sending a snarky reply her way, but I don't. Let her stew in there a while. She'll calm down when she sees that I'm right. No matter how weak Mum was with Dad, she was never weak when it came to disciplining me. At the time I hated her for it, called her all sorts of things. But Mum is still in my life. She may be a little screwed up sometimes, but who the hell isn't?

I grab my empty wine glass from my bedroom and take it downstairs to the kitchen.

Tonight I won't be drowning my sorrows.

Tonight I'll be celebrating an overdue victory.

12

Thea has missed the bus again. She hasn't said a word to me since she got in the car. Sleeping on it clearly hasn't softened the mood.

Was I too rough on her last night?

Maybe, but it's too late to back down now. Thea will grow up a normal, happy person. And someday she'll look back on this and thank me for coming down so hard on her. It won't be tomorrow—or even next year. But one day.

"Aren't you going to eat that?" I ask her as she stares at a slice of buttered toast. "It's going to get cold."

"I'm not hungry," she drones without looking at me.

Another breakfast skipped. I glance at her cheekbones; they're far more noticeable than usual.

"Come on, Thea. You have to eat something. You've got a whole day of school ahead of you. You won't learn anything on an empty stomach."

Thea pulls out a napkin from the glove compartment and wraps it around the toast, then crushes it into a ball.

"Well *that's* a waste of food," I point out, shaking my head in disgust. "You know, there are millions of starving children out in Africa."

"Fine," she replies, stuffing the napkin into the centre cup-holder, "*you* can send it to them."

"That's not a very nice attitude to have."

Thea glares at me with her devil stare. "Whose fault is that, then?"

I almost shout at her, tell her not to talk to her mother like that. But I don't. Instead, I hold my tongue, take a moment, and then force a smile. "You have a nice day in school, sweetheart."

Thea climbs out of the car, throws her school bag over her shoulder and then turns to me, her pale skin now a shade of red, clearly about to say something she'll regret. But instead, she slams the door, so I quickly lower the passenger window. "Have a great day," I shout to her as she storms off. "And I'll see you after school. Don't forget—straight home because you're grounded."

She doesn't retaliate; she just keeps walking until she reaches the school gates, disappearing into the crowds of teenagers.

I let out a long exhale of relief; unsure whether or not I just got a second victory.

Either way, I need a glass of wine.

The TV's on in the living room but it might as well be static. I'm too pissed off to take any of it in. It's almost six and Thea's still not home. I've called everyone I can think of and no one's seen her. I've been to McDonald's, the shopping centre, her friend's house. *Nothing.*

Where the hell is that girl?

My blood feels like acid in my veins. There'll be no more Mrs Nice Guy when she walks in. If she thinks she can test me, she's out of her bloody mind. I'll ground her until she's eighteen if that's what it takes to keep her safe. That's what Mum would have done to me; that's what I should have done to Ivy. Thea needs me to be a firm mother, not some pushover disguised as one of her friends. I won't fail her.

I *can't* fail her.

Shit, I bet she's with that *fucking boy.* That *Jared.* I wish I had his *bloody address!* If he lays a *finger* on my girl, I swear to God he'll be sorry.

I finish the bottle of wine and then go into the kitchen. Reaching into the cupboard, I pull out another and set it down on the worktop. I glance at the back door. Another hour and I'll track down where Jared lives. *Then* she'll be embarrassed. No thirteen-year-old wants to be dragged out kicking and screaming by their mother. I know I would have been mortified if Mum had done that to me.

An image of Callum suddenly pops in my head.

I only met the bastard twice—once at the front door, and the second at the funeral. I could have killed him, right there, in front of everyone. But what would have been the point? Ivy was dead and nothing would have brought back that innocent little girl. Anger and regret are worthless emotions. But there's hope for Thea. A second chance. And this time things will be different.

I pull out the corkscrew from the cutlery drawer and open the bottle. Just as I make my way out of the kitchen, I hear the back door open.

Thea's home.

The grip around the bottle tightens. *Keep it together, Sarah.* "Where the hell have you been?"

"With friends," Thea cagily replies, avoiding eye contact.

She tries to slip past me towards the hallway, but I grab her arm. "Don't lie to me!"

"I'm not lying," she slurs, trying desperately to pull her arm free. Is she drunk? Stoned?

I catch a glimpse of her eyes—*they're bloodshot*.

"What's wrong with your eyes?" I ask her, but I already know the answer. I saw it countless times on Ivy.

She starts to squirm frantically like a captured worm. "Get off me, Mum—*you're hurting me.*"

"What have you taken?" I ask her, trying my best to get a better look at her face.

"Nothing!" she snaps as she slips from my grasp and races towards the stairs.

I chase after her. "You get back here, right now!"

"Leave me alone!"

"I called your friends. They told me they hadn't seen you since school. So come on, *out with it*. You've been taking drugs with Jared—*haven't you?*"

Thea bolts up the stairs, clearly avoiding my question—which only *proves* that I'm not paranoid. "I haven't taken any drugs," she points out. "I'm just tired, that's all."

"Your eyes are bloodshot and you're slurring your words. I'm not stupid."

At the top of the stairs, Thea stops and glowers down at me. "*Slurring?* You're one to talk!"

"And whose fault is that? I've been sat in that living room, waiting for you to get home for three hours. *Three bloody hours!* For all I knew you could have been lying in a ditch somewhere. *Dead!* I almost called the police!"

Thea storms off towards her bedroom. "Well next time just call them! At least then maybe they'll *lock you up!*" She slams the door hard; the sound ripples around the house.

"*Yeah*—and you can stay in your bloody room," I shout, "because you're *grounded for another week!*"

"Good!" I hear Thea scream from her room.

I look down at my hands; they're shaking again. Not even two bottles can steady them. Returning to the kitchen, I grab the wine and take it back into the living room. As I pour myself a glass, all I can think about is Thea, sitting in some grotty flat with Jared, smoking God-knows-what. I gulp down a huge mouthful of wine and pick up the TV remote to channel surf. *Boys. Drugs.* Is that why she's so thin? Is she hooked already? I take a long exhale to try and settle my nerves, but it does nothing. Thea is turning into Ivy. I can see it from a mile off. No matter what I say, no matter how different I do things, she's still her sister—through and through.

I take my finger off the remote when I see that *Ghostbusters* is showing on Channel five. A tiny smile somehow forms on my lips. Ivy's favourite movie. But then I start to cry, and I can't stop the tears flooding out, no matter how much wine I swallow.

13

Mum's texted me three times already. She's asked me if I'd pop 'round the house in the morning. Dad must be still breathing. She'd be straight here if anything had happened. Mum just wants the blood. I'm still unsure whether or not to tell her that I have it. And now is not the time to bug me about anything. I've got enough on my plate.

It's past eight and Thea still hasn't come out of her room. She's obviously stewing in there, thinking of ways to murder me. Christ, I bet she's got my face on a dartboard.

I imagine her sitting on her windowsill, puffing on a joint, or sniffing lines of coke off her desk. The thought makes my chest ache.

I can't go through all that again.

Swallowing the last from my wine glass, I think

about going upstairs, ransacking her bedroom for drugs. But I don't. I can't; I'm too numb to move. I don't know if it's the wine or the fear that I might actually find something.

"Fucking hell!" I shout in frustration, slamming my fist down on the arm of the sofa. *If that bastard has got my little girl hooked, I swear to God I'll crush his skull with my bare hands.*

I'm moments away from smashing this wine glass, so I take a few deep breaths to calm down

Even though I've never even seen Jared, all I can picture is Callum. With that God-awful Tea-cosy hat on his head, those ridiculously tight black jeans, straight out of Mick Jagger's wardrobe, and that vacant, permanently-stoned expression on his *stupid face.*

Stop it, Sarah!

Jared is *not* Callum.

And Thea is *not* Ivy.

I push away another rush of tears, and I get up off the couch, heading for the kitchen. Stumbling drunkenly along the hallway, using the wall for support, I listen out for Thea, but all I hear is the faint sound of her TV.

Inside the kitchen, I open the cupboard to grab

another bottle of wine only to find it empty. *Shit*, I'm all out.

Bugger.

Maybe there's some vodka left over from Christmas. Opening the cupboard next to the oven, I spot the bottle straight away. I hate spirits, but beggars can't be choosers. Reaching in, I notice the jar of hot chocolate. I can't remember the last time Thea and I had one. Probably last year when she came second in the hundred-metre sprint. Jesus, she was like a whippet that day. I've never seen her move so quickly. Ivy was fast—especially when she was young—but nothing like this. I was so proud of her.

I'm already way too drunk to start on the vodka. Hot chocolate sounds great. I pull out the jar and pour a heaped spoonful into the two mugs, flick the switch on the kettle, and wait for it to boil. I don't want to argue with her anymore; I'm too tired. And I've said what needed to be said. I fill the mugs with the hot water and stir them. Marshmallows! There should still be some here. I pull out the biscuit-tin from the cupboard and see a small packet. Yes! Inspecting the bag, I can't see an expiration date, but I'm sure they'll be fine. I dig my hand in, pluck out a handful, and then drop a few in each mug. I stand back and stare at my creation with slightly blurred vision.

Nothing says *truce* like a steaming cup of hot chocolate.

Slowly, I make my way along the hallway and up the stairs. Carrying hot drinks is hard enough, but even worse with a bellyful of red wine. Thank God I didn't have any of that vodka. On the landing, I manage to spill a little from each mug, so I quickly sip each top. *Please don't let her be still pissed off with me.* Reaching her bedroom door, I go to call her name but then stop when I hear something. A voice.

A boy's voice.

I almost lose my grip on the drinks as a wave of anger envelops my body. Setting the mugs down on the small corner table, I burst into her room. The lights are off. I flick the switch and immediately lock eyes on the bed. Thea scrambles to get the quilt over her, trying desperately to cover her exposed chest. There's a blond boy lying next to her on the bed, fifteen, sixteen, his eyes wide open in shock as he frantically reaches for his jeans on the floor.

"What the hell is this?" I scream; both fists clenched in rage.

"*Mum, it's not what you think,*" Thea pleads. But

it's too late. She can reel off every cliché in the book, but it won't undo a thing.

"Get the fuck out of this house!" I shout to the boy as he grabs his jeans from the floor and pulls them under the quilt. "Right now!"

"*Please, Mum,*" Thea sobs, "*he just came over to talk. We just fell asleep. Nothing happened, I swear.*"

"Do you think I was born yesterday?" I ask, grinding my teeth. "Do you?"

The boy leaps out of bed wearing just his jeans and socks. He scans the room, clearly looking for the rest of his clothes.

I see his t-shirt on the floor by my feet. Scooping it up, I throw it at him. He catches it and slips it on. "Get out now!"

"I can't find my shoes," he says, his eyes darting around the room.

"I don't give a *shit* about your fucking shoes," I say. "You can walk home without them. Now out!"

He scurries past me, but stops in the doorway. "I'll call you tomorrow, babe," he says as if this was nothing but a minor inconvenience, something to laugh about in school.

So I drive my fist into his face.

The little prick cries out in pain, cupping his

bleeding nose with both hands. *Who's laughing now you dirty pervert!*

"Mum!" Thea screams. "What have you done?"

I spot a pair of white trainers behind the door. "Here's your fucking shoes," I say, ramming them into his bare chest. "Now piss off!"

The boy darts across the landing, one hand on his nose, the other holding his shoes by the laces. I follow him down the stairs and watch him scuttle out the front door like some frightened animal. By the time I return to Thea's room, she's already dressed in her pyjamas, sitting on the bed, crying into her palms.

"You punched him!" she yells. "Why would you do that?"

Standing in the doorway, I shake my head. How can she be so naïve? Did she really think that I'd put up with something like this? "You promised me that you wouldn't make the same mistakes Ivy made," I say. "Well look at where we are now."

"You're horrible!" she screams at the top of her voice.

"Good! I'm not here to be your friend. I'm your mother, and letting you have sex with some boy— while you're still a *child*—is completely out of the question."

"But I'm *not* a child! I'm thirteen years old. I'm a *teenager*! When are you going to let me live a normal life?"

I let out a short laugh. "A normal life! This isn't normal behaviour. You can't go letting boys just take advantage of you. You'll only end up getting hurt —*or worse.*"

"You can't stop me seeing him!"

"Oh yes I bloody can," I say, smugly, as I grab Thea's mobile phone from her bedside cabinet.

Frantically, Thea crawls across the bed towards me. "That's mine!" she yells, trying to snatch it from my hand.

"I'm confiscating this," I say, stepping back, away from her reach. "I won't let you mess up your life anymore."

Thea gets up from the bed and tries to grab it again. "Give it back! You can't do that! We were only kissing. *Honestly, Mum.*"

Putting the phone behind my back, I hold out my hand to stop her getting any closer. "It's too late, Thea. You're not getting this back until you grow up."

"I hate you!" she screams, still trying to steal the phone from my hand. "I wish you were *dead!*"

Thea suddenly freezes, clearly shocked at what just came out of her mouth.

But she can't possibly be as shocked as me.

Thea's room falls deathly silent.

For once we're both lost for words, my throat and mouth dry.

"*I'm sorry, Mum,*" she says, bursting into tears again. "*I didn't mean that. It just slipped out.*"

I don't answer. I can't. My brain is empty, clouded by alcohol and dismay. So I say nothing, just walk out with the phone, heading for my bedroom. Thea doesn't follow. Just before I step inside, I notice the two mugs of hot chocolate, sitting on the table, the marshmallows melting into a soup of creamy sugar. It's only hot chocolate, but the sight still bites at my heart. I close my bedroom door, too drained even to slam it, and lie on my bed, wondering how the hell that little shit got in? Did he slip past me? No way. Up the drainpipe and through Thea's window.

Dirty fucking pig!

I stuff the phone into my jeans pocket, close my eyes, and then start to cry again.

14

I wake to the sound of tapping on my door.

Did I fall asleep? No, impossible. I only closed my eyes for a second. I check the clock on the bedside cabinet: 9:40 P.M.

I rub my eyes, the effects of the alcohol seemingly much worse, and then swing my legs off the bed and onto the carpet.

There's another tap on the door.

"Come in," I say, croakily. I cough hard to clear my throat.

The door opens, and Thea is standing in the doorway; her eyes and lips red and puffy. The girl's been crying her heart out. A sudden wash of guilt comes over me. Did I overreact?

No, of course I didn't.

Thea steps inside the room, the corners of her

lips hanging low. I think she's about to cry again. "Come here," I say, holding out my arms. She bursts into tears and rushes over to me. I hug her tightly as we sit on the edge of the bed.

"*I'm sorry, Mum,*" Thea sobs, her words muffled by my shoulder. "*I didn't mean what I said. I was angry.*"

We pull out of the hug at the same time. "I know that, honey," I say, holding her hand. "And I'm sorry, too. I shouldn't have hit him. I suppose we were both angry."

"I know he shouldn't have come over. It was only meant to be for two minutes. I think he thought it would be romantic if he climbed the drainpipe to my window."

"Well, maybe in a few years it will be. But right now you're just too young for things like that. Life isn't a movie, Thea. At that age, all boys are interested in is sex. It's illegal for a bloody good reason."

"Okay, Mum," Thea replies, but her eyes suggest that she thinks the exact opposite. She'll get there though. One step at a time.

I kiss her on the cheek. "I hate fighting with you, Thea."

"Me, too."

"You're all I have left."

She hugs me again. "You don't have to worry about me, Mum. I can look after myself."

Smiling, I stare at her with pride, wondering how the hell she grew up so fast. "I don't doubt it," I tell her.

Thea gets up. "I'm going to bed now. I'm a little tired."

"Yeah. Me too."

She leans down and kisses me on the cheek. "Good night, Mum."

"Goodnight," I reply, beaming. "Sleep tight."

She makes her way over to the doorway, but then stops and turns to me. "Oh, and I'm sorry about the hot chocolates. They must be cold by now."

"Don't worry about it. I can always make more."

A giant smile spreads across Thea's beautiful face. "That'd be nice."

"No problem. Why don't you get yourself into bed and I'll bring a mug in for you. How does that sound?"

"Thanks," she says, heading for her bedroom.

When I hear her door close, I breathe a sigh of relief. I didn't expect Thea to be so quick to forgive me. After all, I did probably break her boyfriend's nose. Oh well. I'm just thankful we finally had it out with each other. Sometimes it takes shit like this to realise that things need to change.

Still a little unsteady on my feet, I walk over to the wardrobe mirror. I stare at my face, my eyes. I almost don't recognise the person looking back at me. Have I always had bags under my eyes? I prod the loose skin hanging under my chin. And when did I grow a double bloody chin?

It's the booze. It's got to stop. Thea's right: how am I meant to be a good mother if I'm half-cut all the time.

I rub my tired eyes and release a loud yawn. Just as I do, the photo frame on the chest of drawers catches my eye. I pick it up and stare at it with a smile. It's a picture of when the three of us went to Turkey. It was easily my favourite holiday. Cost me an arm and a leg, but it was worth every penny. Ivy seems so happy too. Those last few years—I can't remember her smiling once. But here, she looks like she doesn't have a care in the world. We all do. And Thea—she's so young in this. She must have been about four years old, but she looks like a baby. I shake my head in astonishment. Where does the time go? Thea's already in secondary school, already has a boyfriend. How the hell did that happen? I feel like I've leaped forward ten years, without even knowing. I can feel myself welling up a little. I don't want to cry anymore, so I kiss the photo, and then put it back down.

Hot chocolates all round, I think.

I leave the bedroom and pick up the disused mugs from the table, and then walk downstairs to the kitchen. *Who needs wine, anyway.* Flicking the switch on the kettle, I pull out two fresh mugs from the cupboard and drop in the cocoa powder. After a minute or so, when the kettle has boiled, I start to pour the water into the mugs. Just as I'm about to grab a handful of marshmallows, I feel something vibrate in my pocket. Reaching in, I feel Thea's phone. I forgot I still had this. Pulling it out, I see that she's had a Facebook message. It's from Jared. My body starts to grit. Should I read it?

No. Don't do it, Sarah.

But then, as if running on autopilot, I push the Facebook icon to read the message.

Jared: '*Hi babe. Tonight was pretty fucked up. I'm sorry if I got you into trouble.*'

I think about racing back upstairs to Thea's room,

confiscating the iPad as well, but instead I watch the screen as each message pops up.

Thea: *'Tell me about it. Mum took my phone. DISAS-TER!!! I'm using the iPad instead. How's the nose? X.'*

Jared: *'Well it's stopped bleeding, so that's a plus.'*

Thea: *'You poor baby xxxx.'*

Jared: *'So what did she say when I left? I bet she went ape shit?'*

Thea: *'Yeah. But it's sorted now. I apologised, and now she's downstairs making me a hot chocolate.'*

Jared: *'Really! Even though she caught you with your top off?'*

Thea: '*Yep. I can handle Mum. She's drunk. She likes to shout a lot, but it's all bark and no bite.*'

Jared: '*Well that's good. Are you still up for Sunday? You're not having second thoughts?*'

Thea: '*No chance. I'm in one 100%. Now more than ever! X.*'

Jared: '*Do you think your Mum will come looking for you? I mean, she seems pretty fucking crazy to me.*'

Thea: '*Yeah, she'll come. And she'll send an army looking for us.*'

Jared: '*And that doesn't put you off?*'

Thea: '*No. It'll be hard and upsetting for a while, but I have to do this. If I stay here then I'm never going to get a normal life. I'll be fourteen in a few months. I should be allowed to have a boyfriend and a sober mother.'*

Jared: *'That's good to know. I love you x.'*

Thea: *'I love you too. I'll message you tomorrow x.'*

Jared: *'Okay, babe. Sleep tight. Don't let the bedbugs bite.'*

Thea: *'Ha. Two seconds with my mother and already you've lost your mind. Nite xxx.'*

Staring down at the phone, I suddenly feel light-headed. Was all that just a sick, twisted joke to get back at me? It must be! Thea would never run away from home. No matter how bad things got. We stick together in this family. We don't run from our problems. We face them head on.

I have to sit down on the kitchen chair, rereading

the messages, hoping, *praying*, that I misinterpreted them. My hand starts to shake. I feel nauseous. I read the messages again; this time they feel even more torturous. *She can't leave me. She's all I've got left. I'd rather* die *than lose her.* I scroll down to read the older messages, hoping to find some clue as to why she would do something like this. Maybe he's putting pressure on my little girl. It can't just be me. If he *is* forcing her, I'll *fucking crush him*. No one hurts my baby. She's not running away. I'll lock her in her room if I have to. Stop her going to that fucking school for starters. She doesn't need that place. I can home-school her. She'll learn more, and be less distracted by druggy boys and worthless friends.

I won't lose another daughter!

I put the phone down on the table and then wrench the cupboard open, pulling out the bottle of vodka. Unscrewing the top, I start to down the liquid, gulping it like water on a hot day. Ignoring the rancid taste, the acid in my throat and stomach, I finish a quarter of the bottle with ease. I belch loudly as I slam the bottle down on the worktop. The vodka does nothing to calm the rage that's bubbling up inside. In fact all it's done is enhance it. I grab Thea's phone again, about to reread the messages, but instead I draw my arm back, and launch the thing across the room. It smashes into pieces the moment it hits the wall, fragments of glass and plastic scattering all over the floor. Heart hammering hard, barely able to catch a breath, I take another huge swig of vodka, slam the bottle down even harder this time, and then storm out of the kitchen.

We'll see who's running away!

Just as my foot hits the first step of the staircase, I stop. I know exactly what will happen if I confront her. Thea will deny it all; tell me that it was just a prank to get back at me. We'll have another screaming match and then we're back to square one. She's already made her mind up. That little fucker of a boyfriend has already snaked his way into her heart, introduced her to drugs —*clawed his way into her bed.* I see Ivy and me sitting in the clinic; the last place I ever thought we'd be. *It still haunts me.* I never wanted her to have the abortion. But what choice did she have? She was fifteen, for Christ's sake! She was scared, hooked on coke, and with a deadbeat boyfriend. I thought that that would be the end of all her problems; I thought getting rid of the baby would make her see the light. But I was wrong. I foolishly imagined that screaming at her would get her to see sense, to leave Callum in the gutter. *I was wrong about that, too.* There's no one in the world that can talk Thea out of leaving Jared and staying here with me. She's too stubborn—just like all the women in this family.

It's our curse.

So what the hell am I suppose to do? Let her walk out. If I lock her in, she's bound to slip away. And all I'd be giving her is another reason to run away. But Thea's strong and wise. She'll soon see that this is stupid. She's just a baby; she's got no money, no street smarts. She'll get killed out there in the real world.

Like Ivy.

No!

I bang my fist down onto the banister in anger, the force and sound travelling up to the landing.

I feel sick so I sit down on the stairs, the vodka already taking effect. The entire house feels like it's caught in a tornado, forcing me to close my eyes. And there's Jared again, only this time there's no look of terror on his face. This time there's a huge grin as he cuts up a small white rock with a razor blade, turning it into powder. Thea is next to him; her beautiful blue eyes glazed over and bloodshot;

her young thin body, starved of life, drained from the inside.

And now Thea is holding the razor as Jared sits next to her on the bed. Her eyes are barely open; too messed up to know what she's doing. She hovers the blade over her wrist.

No. I don't want to see this.

Jared strokes her blonde hair as she presses the blade against her skin.

She starts to cut.

No!

My eyes spring open in horror.

Thea is mine!

Not his!

And with that, I stomp back into the kitchen, slamming my shoulder drunkenly against the door-frame. Unable to see straight, I reach for one of the mugs of hot chocolate, but miss the handle completely. I have to strain to focus my vision, but manage to grab it on my second attempt. *I finally know exactly what I have to do.* I hobble across the hallway towards the stairs, spilling some of the drink in the process. *Something that I should have done for Ivy.* Stumbling dangerously up the stairs, I hold on tightly to the banister for support. Snippets of Ivy's funeral start to invade my mind. The massive turn out, the horror of watching them lower my little girl into a dirty grave; Thea and Mum beyond tears, beyond words. I almost fall into my bedroom, spilling more hot chocolate over the carpet. I close the door and then set the mug down on the bedside cabinet. *I'd rather die than see another daughter stuffed into a wooden box.* I yank my sock drawer open, reach inside and sift through all the loose socks. My fingers touch the vial of vampire blood, so I pull it out.

This is for your own good, my princess. The real world is a loathsome place. There's too much pain outside. In here, with me, is safe. I'll protect you from the monsters, and the pain. You won't get sick, and you'll never die— because your mother loves you. *More than anything.*

I twist open the lid and pour the blood into Thea's hot chocolate. There's no spoon, so I use a pen to stir the mug until the dark red colour mixes with the chocolate. Images of Thea and Ivy flood my thoughts as I stare at the contaminated drink— before life got dark and cruel, a happy time before Callum and Jared *infected* my babies.

My vision still blurred, I leave the bedroom and walk over to Thea's door, this time making sure that I don't spill a single drop. I take a few deep breaths, trying to sober up, and then knock the door. Thea opens it straight away, smiling. It's fake. *How could she be smiling when she's so close to leaving me?*

"Thanks, Mum," she says when she spots the hot chocolate. "Looks great."

I hesitate for a moment, but then hand her the drink, returning a smile. *But mine is real.*

"No marshmallows?" she asks as she sets the mug down on her bedside cabinet.

Shit. Marshmallows. I forgot. "Sorry, sweetheart," I slur, using the doorframe to hold me up straight. "It slipped my mind. Must be out of practice."

"It's okay, Mum. I was only teasing. It's fine without them."

"Next time," I say with another smile. "Enjoy."

"Aren't you having one, Mum?"

"No. I'm fine. Trying to cut down on sugar." I kiss her on the cheek. "Goodnight. I'll see you in the morning."

"Goodnight, Mum," Thea replies, closing the door. "Thanks."

I stop and turn to her. "Drink up now. You wouldn't want it to go cold."

"I will. Love you."

"Love you, too."

She closes the door and an all-consuming sense

of relief washes over me. Not guilt. Not regret. Just a feeling of hope.

I'm tired, drunk beyond belief, and I feel queasy. I need to sleep off all this booze. But instead of stopping outside my room, I find myself standing by Ivy's door. And like a woman possessed by some supernatural entity, I walk over to the corner table, reach into the glass vase, fish out the skeleton key, and then open the door to Ivy's room. My heart judders a little as I step inside, switching the light on.

Apart from all the cobwebs along the ceiling, the dust and dead moths resting on the cabinets and shelves, everything is exactly as it was that night. The same purple painted walls, dirty clothes, and underwear scattered across the floor. The DVD disk-tray still sticking out with *American Psycho* ready to be played or removed. Her dresser is covered in makeup and pens. The wardrobe doors are hanging half-open. If it weren't for the fact that I knew she was such a messy teenager, then I'd think the place had been ransacked. The only thing that's tidy is her bed. It's the only part of the room that Mum had to tamper with. I sit on it. It's so soft. It's one of Mum's spare mattresses. I told her not to bother replacing Ivy's, but she did it anyway. Even made the bed with fresh sheets and a spare quilt.

On the wall, I notice the water-painting she did of Thea. I can't believe she had it up for so many years. It's beautiful. It truly captures Thea's cheeky spirit. I thought about having it in my bedroom, framed to the wall. But it belongs in here. It's her talent. She got it from my mother. Art is *not* my forte.

Sitting on the bedside cabinet is a photo of her and her friends in some theme park. I can't remember when it was, but she looks happy. They all do. She must be about thirteen in this judging by her bobbed haircut. I loved that.

Eyelids heavy, I lie down, facing the window; the curtains still open. The room still smells of Ivy. I can't quite put my finger on the scent. It's just...*her*. I imagine how low she must have been to do what she did.

I remember the blood. I can still feel it against my skin as I lay next to her.

"*I love you, Ivy,*" I mumble as my eyes fully close. "*I miss you so much.*"

Pulling the quilt over my body, I smile, even though I'm crying. Tomorrow I'll have a hangover. *A terrible one.* But it won't matter one bit.

Because tomorrow Thea will still be home.

My baby.

For good...

PART IV

THICKER THAN WATER

15

The morning light burns its way through my eyelids. I fight hard to keep them closed, but I can't. As soon as I open them, as soon as the world reforms around me, the pain in my head kicks in, followed by the rancid taste of vodka in my mouth. I rub my forehead and eyes, and then sit up in bed.

Where the hell am I?

My stinging eyes scan my surroundings. *Ivy's bedroom.* How the hell did I end up here?

But then I remember being blind drunk, getting the key from the vase, and walking in. I must have just passed out on the bed.

I see myself throwing Thea's phone across the kitchen, breaking it to bits against the wall. Why?

Thea's Facebook messages. *She's planning to run away with Jared.*

"Shit!" Did I shout at her? I must have.

I see myself making her a hot chocolate, swaying up the stairs to give it to her. Why? Did we make up? Did I talk her out of leaving?

But then it hits me! And I can't breathe, the walls around me closing in—*because I remember everything.*

I leap off the bed in a panic.

Thea!

What the fuck have I done?

I race out of the room, along the landing to Thea's bedroom. *Please, God—tell me that I just dreamed it! Please tell me I didn't poison my daughter!* Grabbing the door handle, I barge my way inside the room. "Thea!" I blurt out. The bed is empty. She's gone!

On the bedside cabinet, I spot the mug.

It's empty!

Oh dear God, no!

Picking up the mug, I see that every last drop is gone. All that remains is a thin layer of dried chocolate stuck to the inside.

I feel sick. But not from the alcohol, swimming around in my blood. I wish it were.

"Thea!" Where the hell is she?

Has she turned already?

Racing along the landing, I quickly check my bedroom. She's not here. I check the bathroom as well. Deserted. Practically soaring down the entire length of the staircase, I land on the hallway and then bolt into the kitchen. *Where the hell are you?*

"Morning, Mum," Thea says from the table.

Almost choking with relief, I grab hold of the wall, with the other hand over my hammering heart.

She's just eating corn flakes. She's still Thea.

Oh, thank God!

"Did you drink the hot chocolate?" I ask, unable to contain the panic in my voice. *Of course she bloody drank it! The mug was empty!*

"Yeah," she replies. "Why?"

"All of it?"

"Yeah," she replies with a confused frown. "Of course I did. What's wrong?"

"What time did you drink it? How long has it been in your system?"

"Why?"

"Just answer me!"

Thea's eyes broaden in shock at my sudden outburst.

"I'm sorry, sweetheart," I say in a forced calm voice. "Just tell me." I pull out a chair from under the table and sit down, my hands over hers, preventing her from eating.

There's that frown again. She thinks I've lost it.

"I drank it last night. As soon as you left my room," she replies, pulling her hand out of mine. "You're being weird. Are you still drunk?"

I shake my head. "No, I'm not drunk. I just need to know if you're okay."

"Why? What's wrong with the hot chocolate? It tasted fine."

"Nothing's wrong with it."

"Then what's the big deal?"

I think for a moment, trying to come up with a suitable lie. *I can't possibly tell her the truth.* "It's the milk I used to make it," I lie—the very first thing that pops into my spinning mind. "I think it's gone off."

Thea looks at me in revulsion, then down at her cereal. "Thanks, Mum," she says with a wince. "I've already eaten half a bowl." Dropping the spoon into the milk, she gets up off her chair and takes her cereal over to the sink. "That's disgusting."

I can't stop my heart pounding, my hands shaking. I try to will them to settle, but nothing happens. The room starts to swirl; my stomach roils.

I'm going to be sick!

Jumping up, I get to the sink in a split second and throw up all over the dirty dishes.

"Bloody hell, Mum!" she says, leaping out of the way in fright. "You've got to stop drinking. It's not good for you."

Holding onto the edge of the sink, I spit out the last remaining vomit. My stomach feels no better. I put the cold tap on, fill up my palm with water and then rinse my mouth.

"Are you okay?" Thea asks, her hand on my back as I lean over the sink. "I've never seen you like this."

I rub some water over my face and leave the tap running to swill the vomit-covered dishes. "I'm fine. Must be something I ate."

"Maybe it's the milk. Am I gonna get ill?"

"No," I reply, shaking my head. "You'll be fine."

How the fuck would I know?

Glancing over at the digital clock on the microwave, I start to count the hours since she drank the blood. It's 10:03 A.M., so it's been over eight hours. Surely something would have happened by now. I stare into Thea's eyes, looking for any sort of evidence that something has changed. I can't see anything; she has the same blue eyes; her skin is fair, but no lighter than usual.

Sunlight!

The blinds are still closed. I race over to them and yank the string until they fully open. The kitchen instantly brightens as the sun glares through the glass. I quickly turn to Thea, but all I see is a thirteen-year-old girl standing in the middle of the kitchen, looking at me with eyes filled with perplexity—like I've just gone insane overnight.

I think I have. No wonder she wants to leave.

I shield my eyes from the bright glow of the sun. Thea has barely flinched though.

It was fake. *Of course it was.* I bet Kate's dealer just gave her a vial of watered-down ketchup. I've been totally scammed—*Thank God for that.*

"There's something wrong with you," Thea says, sighing loudly as she shakes her head. She then makes her way out of the kitchen.

"Where are you going?" I ask, still struggling to hide the alarm in my voice. *What's there to be alarmed about? She's absolutely fine. I'm sure of it.*

"To watch TV," she replies with a scowl, stopping at the doorway. "Is that all right with you? Or am I grounded from the living room as well?"

I hardly register the sarcasm in her tone as she leaves the kitchen. I think about chasing after her, but I stay put, staring at the empty doorway.

Should I take her to the hospital, just in case?

No, there's no point. She's fine. It's been eight hours. If there *was* anything bad in her system, then it's gone now.

And what if the police found out what I did to her? They'd arrest me. Then I'd never get to see my little girl again. She'd be out the door with Jared even before I got to court.

She's fine.

I sit down; still not ready to feel relief. The only relief that I feel is that the blood was fake.

To hell with the money. I'll pay Mum back somehow.

And to hell with Dad, too.

If Mum wants vampire blood—she can get it herself next time.

16

1 0:07 P.M. Way past Thea's bedtime. But after the monstrous morning I've had, I'm sure a late night is the least of my worries.

We've been watching a movie for the past hour. I don't even know what it's called. Something about a beach house and an old witch. Thea says that I've already seen this, but for the life of me I can't remember. I have a very selective memory. Moments in my childhood, Ivy and Thea growing up, I can see them in 3D. People's names or movies I've supposedly seen? Not so much.

Thea has her head resting against my shoulder, and I have my arm around her. After the madness of last night, with Jared and everything, this is the last thing I thought we'd be doing today. But here we are, like old times, huddled up on the couch on a

Saturday night. Bliss. I haven't even drunk a single drop of wine, too. Don't know if I've turned over a new leaf, or that I'm still in a state of shock. Either way, I'm just glad that Thea is still Thea.

But the messages?

She's still planning to run away with Jared. That can't have changed overnight. Can it?

Maybe she's not going. Maybe it was just the vodka, making me read into things too much.

No. The messages were crystal clear. She wants to leave.

But I won't allow it!

The movie finishes just as I let out a long, theatrical yawn. "Come on then, sweetheart," I say, switching the TV off with the remote, "time for bed."

"What time is it?" Thea asks.

"Late. So come on," I reply, getting off the couch, "up you get."

Thea groans, but then follows me up and out of the living room.

I switch all of the lights off and then we both head upstairs.

Just outside Ivy's room, Thea stops. "Have you been inside?" she asks, peeking through the slightly ajar door.

"Yeah. Last night. I just had a look around."

"Really? That's good," she says with a smile. "Can I go in?"

"Of course you can, but not right now. Tomorrow. We'll both go in, maybe sort through some of her stuff. How does that sound?"

"Yeah. Okay."

I usher her away from the door, towards her own. "Now bed, madam. You need your beauty sleep."

Outside her room, I give her a kiss on the cheek. Just as I move away, I take her in my arms and pull her in for a hug.

"Mum, you're squishing me," Thea playfully says, her words muted by my shirt.

"Tough," I reply, squeezing even harder. "It's your own fault for being so huggable."

After a few more seconds, I finally let her go. Thea beams. It sends a warm sensation around me, drowning out my craving for a glass of red.

"Goodnight," I say as Thea steps inside her room. "Sweet dreams."

"You too. Goodnight," Thea replies, slowly closing her door.

I stand outside her room for maybe half a minute, trying to keep the guilt of last night at bay. I can't let myself dwell on it. What's done is done and there's no going back. I made a mistake, and thank God I didn't pay for it.

Tomorrow is a new day in the Wilkes household.

I blow a kiss to Thea through the door, and then head off to bed.

Goodnight my angel.

Don't let the bedbugs bite.

I hear the rain hammer against the bedroom window. Don't know what time it is. Can't face opening my eyes to check the bedside clock. Must be around 2:00 A.M. I've had broken sleep all night, dreaming about Ivy. They used to be nightmares. But not these. For the first time in years, these dreams were happy ones. I don't know what's changed. Maybe finally going into her room? Whatever the reason, I feel like I may have turned a corner. It's taken me a while, and I'm not likely ever to be able to fully move on. But it's a start.

I focus on my breathing as I try to drift off. It's hard with the storm outside, but I love the sound it makes against the glass.

After a few minutes, I open my eyes to check the clock. For a moment my vision is too blurred to see the display, but then I see that it's 2:05 A.M. Jesus, I was pretty close. You can't beat your own body clock.

Just as I start to rest my head back on the pillow, I jump with fright; my heart beats violently against my chest.

There's a figure—*it's standing at the end of my bed.*

Grasping the edge of the quilt tightly, I start to see the outline of hair; long hair to delicate shoulders. The lightning strikes, lighting up the room in an instant.

It's Thea.

Switching on the bedside lamp, I breathe a sigh of relief.

What the hell is wrong with me? Who else could it be? A bloody ghost?

"Hi, sweetheart," I say, sitting up against the headboard. "Is everything all right?"

She doesn't answer; her vacant eyes locked down on the bed, but not on me.

"Thea?" I ask. "Are you okay?"

Still no reply.

Is she sleepwalking?

No. She's never done it before.

"Thea?" I repeat, a little louder this time. "Can you hear me?"

She slowly lifts her head; her eyes line up with

mine. "I can't sleep," she mumbles.

Pulling some of the quilt from the mattress, I pat the empty side of my double bed. "Jump in then," I say with pretend reluctance. But she knows I'm a sucker for company, especially with weather like this.

Thea slowly walks around to the side of the bed and climbs in. She rests the back of her head on the pillow and pulls the quilt up to her chest.

"Try to get some sleep now, honey," I say, softly. "You need your rest." I lean over and kiss her on the cheek. "Goodnight."

She doesn't reply as I turn off the lamp

Feeling exhausted, I close my eyes. Sleep is coming; I can feel it.

After maybe ten or so minutes, I open my eyes. The storm seems to have settled. The moonlight, working its way through the curtains is the only light in the room. I turn to Thea. Her eyes are still wide open, staring up at the ceiling. I think about saying something, but what's the point? She'll sleep when she sleeps.

There's nothing strange about a little girl struggling to sleep.

We've all been there. It's perfectly normal.

She's not a vampire...

17

I've been up since eight. Thea's still asleep in my bed. But I couldn't disturb her this morning after the night she had. She looked so peaceful lying there next to me, hugging the quilt tightly like a soft toy.

The storm has passed, and the sun is shining: a perfect Sunday morning for pancakes and syrup. I haven't made these in years; Thea's favourite. I cook about six mini ones first, leaving the rest of the batter in the jug. If she wants more, then I'll make them later. I've searched the cupboard, and all I could find was golden syrup; no maple. Oh well, that will have to do until I've gone shopping.

I lay the pancakes on a large plate and set them down on the kitchen table, next to the orange juice. God knows why I'm in such an optimistic mood after all the drama. And I have no illusion that pancakes or cutting back on wine will suddenly change Thea's feelings about running away. But at least it's a start.

I walk out into the hallway and call up to Thea. It's almost eleven; she should be up by now.

She doesn't respond.

I try again and still nothing. *She's just tired, that's all.*

I walk up the stairs to my bedroom. Poking my head through the open door, I see Thea still fast asleep, with the quilt covering most of her face.

"Thea," I whisper. "Are you hungry? I've made pancakes."

She doesn't flinch.

"Thea," I whisper again. "*Wakey, wakey, sleepy head*. It's late."

Still nothing.

I walk over to her side of the bed and sit on the edge. "Sweetheart," I whisper, trying to repress the fear in my gut.

Don't say it. Don't even think it. She's fine.

"I've made us pancakes."

No movement.

"Thea!" I say, almost shouting, prodding her on the shoulder. "Wake up!"

Still nothing.

I reach for her neck to check her pulse. *She's fine, Sarah. Don't panic. Teenagers are meant to sleep in on Sundays.*

The moment my fingers touch her cold skin, she stirs.

See. Everything's fine.

Sighing in relief, I make my way over to the curtains. "Come on, honey, it's a beautiful day." I pull the curtains apart, the bright morning sun bringing the room to life.

"CLOSE THE FUCKING CURTAINS!" Thea screams at me.

Heart pounding in fright, I turn to her as she pulls the quilt over her head. *Oh shit!* Is this a symptom? My stomach starts to spiral as the thought of infection occupies my head. I try to repress it again, push it as far back as possible—*but it won't budge.* "Don't speak to me like that," I mumble, my words lacking any authority. "I'm your mother."

"Just leave me alone," she says, her voice muffled by the quilt. "*I'm tired.*"

I stare at the bed, unable to decide how to handle this. She's been awake for most of the night. I'll let her sleep.

The blood was fake, Sarah. Nothing has changed.

"Fine," I say in defeat, pulling the curtains

closed, "stay in bed and waste a beautiful Sunday. *Your* loss, *not* mine."

Just as I start to leave the room, I stop at the doorway, taking one last look at the mound of quilt covering Thea.

You're still you.

All this seems so familiar.

I've been sitting in this chair, staring at Thea as she sleeps, for the past three hours. It'll be getting dark soon, and all she's done is stir a few times. Just like her sister. But at least when it was Ivy lying in bed, sleeping off a night of ecstasy or cocaine, she was the one who poisoned herself.

Not me.

I've tried to wake her a few times, but each time she's knocked me back. Even when I offered to order in a pizza.

Wake up, Thea. Come on, sweetheart. Stop scaring Mummy.

I reach over to the chest of drawers and grab my glass of vodka and orange juice. The stress of the day just got a little too much. I've only had two and I still feel guilty—but not surprised. Did I really think that one day off the booze would somehow be enough? How naïve can you get?

Even though I still hate the taste, I finish the glass with little effort. No more vodka today; I want to be sober when she wakes.

18

Thea finally wakes at 6:51 P.M. The curtains are still drawn, but the sun is up.

That's the main thing.

I can't hide the great big grin across my face when she sees me.

"Why are you sitting there?" Thea asks, her words stifled by a giant yawn.

I get up off the chair and sit on the edge of the bed, taking hold of her hand. "Just making sure you're all right. You've been asleep for most of the day."

Frowning, clearly thinking that I'm joking, she leans over and squints at the time on the bedside clock. Her mouth hangs open in disbelief when she sees how late it is. "Oh my God. It's nearly seven. I can't believe it." She sits back against the headboard, clearly in a state of shock. "How did I get in your bed? Did you carry me in?"

"Don't you remember? You came in here at two this morning, telling me you couldn't sleep."

Thea shakes her head, pursing her lips. "No, I can't remember. Was I sleepwalking?"

"I don't know," I reply with a shrug. "Could've been. You were in a bit of a daze."

"That's weird. I've never done that before. Have I, Mum?"

"Not that I can remember. Your sister did it a couple of times when she was very young."

Thea checks the time again. "Well, this is officially the latest I've ever slept in."

I smile, but it's false. I'm trying my best to push away this horrible foreboding in my gut, but it's as stubborn as I am.

"Hungry?" I ask her, stroking her arm. "I made pancakes."

"Pancakes! Yes, definitely. I'm starving."

We both climb off the bed. I hand Thea my dressing gown from behind the door, and she slips it on. "I'll have to warm them up, though. I made them this morning."

"Sorry, Mum. You should have woken me up. I'll always get up for pancakes."

I follow her out of the bedroom towards the stairs. "Next time I'll try a little harder."

"Bloody hell," I say to Thea as I watch her devour her fifth pancake in a row, "you must be full by now."

Thea shakes her head. "Not yet. I haven't eaten a thing all day, so you better keep them coming."

"That was the last one, but I can make you a sandwich if you want."

With her finger, Thea scoops up the syrup from the plate, and then licks it off. "Only if you don't mind, Mum."

"Of course I don't mind. I'm your mother."

"Thanks."

I take out two slices of bread from the breadbin and lay them out on the chopping board. "Ham and cheese okay?" I ask, opening the fridge and staring at all the empty shelves. Need to go shopping tomorrow.

Thea doesn't answer, so I turn to her. "Ham and cheese?" I ask again just as I see how white her cheeks have gone. "Are you okay, sweetheart?"

Before she can say a word, Thea leaps up from

the table and races out of the kitchen, cupping her mouth.

"What's wrong?" I say, chasing her as she bolts out of the kitchen and up the stairs.

She reaches the top in a second and disappears into the bathroom. I race after her, the sound of vomiting journeying around the house. In the bathroom, I stand behind her, my palm rubbing her back, listening as she wretches and coughs into the toilet.

After a few minutes, she finally stops, lets out a tired groan and then flushes the toilet. She turns to me, eyes bloodshot, the colour in her cheeks still drained. "Feeling any better?" I ask her.

Thea just shakes her head.

"Do you think it was the pancakes?" I ask. *Of course it wasn't the fucking pancakes!*

"I think I'm just going to go to bed," Thea replies croakily, her throat clearly strained.

"That's a good idea. Do you want to sleep in my bed again?"

"No. I'd rather sleep in my room if that's okay."

"All right, sweetheart. It's up to you. I'll bring a pan up in case you're sick again."

"There's no need. I'll use my bin."

"Okay then. Try to get some sleep. If you're still rough tomorrow, I'm calling the doctor."

A doctor? Really? What if he finds something in her blood? They'll call the police.

Thea smiles through dried, cracked lips. "Okay. Goodnight, Mum."

"Goodnight. Call me if you need anything."

Thea ambles across the landing to her bedroom, her head hanging low. I won't need a doctor, anyway. She'll be fine by the morning. It's probably just a bug.

A fucking *bug? You're in denial, Sarah. She's infected.*

Shut up!

Once Thea closes her door, I walk back down to the kitchen. My hand wobbles as I make myself a vodka and orange juice. I might as well finish the bottle. At least it's all gone then.

I take the drink into the living room and sit on the couch. Each sip pushes away the worry. There's a cheesy Sunday night movie on: *Titanic*. That's exactly what I need right now.

I take a huge gulp from my glass and focus on the movie.

What the hell were you thinking? You poisoned your own child! How could you?

Shut up!

I swallow another mouthful.

Just watch the bloody movie.

You could have killed her! She's all you have left in the world!

It was an accident!

I finish the drink.

I know that actress from somewhere. Wasn't she the crazy woman in *Misery*?

You're gonna burn in hell for what you did!

Stop it! Stop it!

STOP IT!

I jump up from the couch and exit the living room.

I need another drink.

Fuck the orange juice!

The movie is almost over. Even after four more drinks, I still managed to follow the plot. The vodka bottle is nearly empty. I won't be buying any more of the stuff; it's too strong.

The TV screen is blurred. I thought for a moment that we needed a new one, but luckily for me, it's just the booze. I need to pee. I've been holding it in for the past hour; just couldn't face getting up off this couch. My bladder can't bear another moment of this torture, so I get up, using the arm of the couch for support. I'm not drunk; I'm just dead tired. It's been a long couple of days.

I haven't heard a peep out of her all night. *I'm sure she's fine.* Climbing the stairs, I grasp the banister tightly, trying desperately to focus on each step. When I reach the summit, I listen out for her. *She's probably fast asleep—exactly what I should be doing right now.* I stumble into the bathroom, lock the door and sit on the toilet. Slumped forward, I think about Thea running away. Is she still thinking about going? We haven't had an argument for a couple of days; maybe she's had a change of heart. I flush the toilet, run my hands under the tap and dry them on the towel. There's still time to change her mind. Still time to convince her that running away is a terrible idea. I exit the bathroom and step onto the landing.

I hear a loud thud—*it came from Thea's room!*

Bolting towards her door, vision now in focus, I hear screaming. Adrenaline surging, I barge inside her bedroom and see the bed empty. And then my eyes drop to the floor to find Thea. She's on her hands and knees, a pool of blood around her—*her head buried deep into someone's throat.* A boy. I race over and grab her by the shoulders—but she won't budge. "Thea!" I shout, pulling even harder. I manage to pry her off the boy, taking with her a mouthful of skin. A jet of blood sprays over the wardrobe and walls. Thea turns to me, hissing through red-stained teeth. "Oh my God! What have you done?"

I freeze when I see what's left of Jared, as he lies on the carpet, body twitching, choking, bleeding to death. Thea quickly mounts him again, sinking her jaws into his neck.

I start to gasp for air, my hands, my entire body convulsing. *This isn't real. It can't be. I've fallen asleep on the couch.*

I try to speak, but my vocal cords no longer function. Whatever noise manages to leave my mouth is drowned out by the sound of sucking.

"*Thea,*" I finally say as I start to creep towards her. "*It's me, honey. It's Mummy.*"

The slurping comes to a sudden halt.

"*Sweetheart,*" I say, slowly reaching for her shoulder, "come away from him." I hold my breath as my juddering hand touches her pyjama top. Thea pulls her mouth away from Jared's throat. "*It's Mummy, sweetheart. Everything's going to be all right.*"

The room becomes still, just the sound of breathing.

Thea tips her head back, a mix of saliva and blood hanging from her chin, and then lets out a loud, painful squeal. I jump back in fright and my head hits the wall.

"*It's Mummy,*" I plead. "*Listen to my voice.*"

Thea springs up onto her feet; the entire front of her body is soaked with blood. Her eyes are locked onto mine, her posture firm like a cat about to pounce.

"*Please,*" I sob, struggling to speak. "*Snap out of it.*"

She doesn't acknowledge my words.

I back away to the side, heading for the doorway. She follows my movement.

I'm a metre away from the landing.

She's getting closer.

"*Please, Thea. I know you're in there. Wake up, honey.*"

She suddenly darts towards me, shrieking like a wild beast. Just before she reaches me, I manage to get onto the landing and slam the door, trapping her inside the bedroom.

With both hands, I grasp the handle tightly as she beats on the door. "*Stop it, Thea! Please!*"

My grip nearly slips as the door moves ever so

slightly. *I need to lock it.* I see the vase on the table; the skeleton key is inside it. But it's too far away.

Should I make a dash for it?

No, she'll get out!

And I can't let her. Not yet.

She's too dangerous.

I feel the sweat run down my face, mixing with the tears. *Keep holding. No matter what.*

Forget about what you've done.

Forget about Jared.

All that can wait.

Just focus on keeping her inside. She'll be calm soon, back to her normal self. And then you can let go. Then it'll be safe. In a few hours.

When the sun comes up.

PART V

BLACK SUN

.

19

There's a golden beam of light travelling across the landing.

Sunrise.

What time is it?

With both hands still clutching the door handle, I manage to check the time on my watch. 6:03 A.M.

On my knees, my head thrashing, I listen out for signs of life through Thea's door. Haven't heard anything for about an hour. That's when she stopped trying to rip the door off its hinges.

She must be sleeping by now.

I thought about calling someone—even the police at one point during the night. But that's not going to happen. Not a chance in hell. They'd kill her, without a second thought—thirteen or not. Calling Mum or Kate crossed my mind, too, but the idea of confessing sends a shudder of loathing through me.

No, I'm her mother, and this is *my* mess, *my* problem. I'll fix it—as I always do. Thea's aggression will pass. I'm sure it's just the early effects of the blood.

Blood.

There was just so much of it. That poor boy.

What the hell was he doing here?

Was he here to take her away from me?

Maybe they got into a fight over it. For all I know, he tried to force her to leave.

That could have triggered the rage.

No! Stop making excuses! I have to accept the facts: Thea tore that boy's throat out because she's infected.

And his death is on *my* hands.

I press my ear to her door. Still silent

I need to get in there, check if she's okay, clean up the blood before anyone comes around snooping.

What do I do about the body? I can't just hide it in the house—the neighbours will smell it.

I'll bury it. In the garden.

Shit, I don't even own a spade.

I'll buy one. Today.

I suck in a lungful of air and slowly take one

hand off the handle. Swallowing hard, I give the door a gentle tap.

No response.

"Thea," I call out softly, tapping the door for a second time.

Still nothing.

I brace for a few seconds before slowly twisting the handle and pushing, still listening out for Thea. The door is stuck. I push again, this time a little harder. The door starts to shift, rubbing against the carpet. What's blocking it? With my shoulder—feet planted firmly on the floor—I slowly manage to push the door open, leaving just enough of a gap to squeeze through.

I can feel my pulse rocket as I carefully step inside the room. When my head is in, immediately I see Thea, propped up against the door.

A shockwave of horror hits me when I don't see her chest move.

Please, God, don't say she's dead. Don't you dare do this to me again.

Don't you fucking *dare!*

Inside the room, I kneel over her still body; the fear of an attack replaced by something much worse. Just as I reach for her neck to check for a pulse, I see her chest suddenly rise.

"*Oh, thank God*," I say under my breath, exhaling in relief.

Should I try to get her into bed? No, best leave her where she is. I can't risk another frenzy. Her pink dressing gown is on the floor, so I lay it over her like a blanket.

For maybe a minute I stare at my baby, fast asleep, pretending that the red on her face and clothes is something else. Maybe grape juice. Or tomato soup.

Not blood.

Never blood.

Turning my head, I see Jared's body on the floor. He looks so young. My stomach spins when I see the state of his throat. He's not twitching anymore, just still, like he's sleeping soundly on the floor.

There's no way he slipped past me last night. He must have used the window again. I need to lock it in case Thea decides to climb out. I dread to think what could happen if she got outside. Avoiding Jared's body, I crawl over the bed to get to the window, holding my breath as the springs squeak loudly. Glancing over my shoulder, I see that Thea is still sleeping, undisturbed by the noise. I twist the tiny key to lock the window and then slip it into my pocket. Crawling back over the bed, I catch another glimpse of Jared. I feel queasy, but I push the feeling to one side and focus on the task at hand: getting this room clean, and disposing of the body.

If I think too hard about it, let the fact that I'm about to bury a teenager in my garden *truly* seep in —then I'll never go through with it.

And I can't let that happen.

I won't let Thea pay for what I've done.

But before I do anything—I need to buy a spade.

20

The last thing I ever thought I'd have to do was lock my own daughter up. But I'm out of options. Yeah, the sun is up and she'll probably sleep all day—but I can't risk it. What if she got confused, stepped outside? She'd burn to death.

They sell spades at work, but I couldn't risk running into someone I know—especially Kate. Didn't think I could face her line of questioning. I'm a terrible liar and I'm bound to confess all as soon as I saw her. I felt guilty enough buying the bloody thing from the DIY shop thirty miles away. For some reason, I felt that a woman buying a spade immediately suggested *murderer*. So I bought a few potted plants and a rake, just in case.

And a few bottles of wine in the shop next door.

Our garden can barely hold the title. There's just

a small wooden shed, a tiny patch of dying grass, and a pathetic, concrete patio section for barbecues. We haven't had a barbecue in years, since even before Thea was born—when Mark was still living with us. Now, it's stained green and covered in weeds.

I enter the shed, breaking a massive cobweb as the stiff wooden door opens. I haven't been in here in ages; it's filled mostly with junk: a rusty lawn-mower, which I haven't used in awhile, a leaf-blower, which I've *never* used, a few boxes, and some cracked plant pots. I prop my new rake against the wall, place the new plant pots on the shelf, and then kneel down to inspect the floor. Maybe I could pull up the wood and bury him underneath. At least in here I can keep the door shut and take as long as I need. I give the floor a tap and quickly come to the conclusion that I haven't got a hope in hell of pulling this wood up.

It has to be the garden, then. I'll just have to be really quiet and pray to God one of the neighbours doesn't see me.

A flash of Jared's torn throat hits me.

What the hell are you doing, Sarah? You can't bury someone in the garden. This is not you. You have to tell someone.

No! This is the only way. Thea comes first. Nothing else matters.

I check my watch: 10:17 A.M. *Need to get busy.*

Just as I step out of the shed, it suddenly dawns on me that I haven't called Thea's school. I race into the house and grab my mobile from the handbag. There are two missed calls from Mum.

Shit! I just remembered! I'm meant to be working tonight! I need to tell them that I'm sick. *Bloody hell,* Mum is coming round later to babysit.

I dial her number; my muscles tighten up as I wait for the call to connect. Don't know why I'm so nervous; it's not like Mum will work out what's happened.

Or would she?

"Hi, Sarah," Mum says through the phone. "I've been trying to call you for a few days. Where've you been hiding?"

"Nowhere," I reply, cagily. "Things have been a little hectic, that's all."

"How's Thea? I haven't seen her in a while."

"She's fine," I reply, desperate to push the conversation on. "I won't need you to babysit tonight. I'm not working. Sorry if it's short notice."

"Oh, right. That's okay. Maybe I'll pop round anyway. I'd love to see Thea."

A jolt of panic hits me. Thank God she can't see my face. "No, Mum. She's sick. She's got a nasty stomach bug. We both have. That's why I'm not working later."

"A stomach bug? Sounds awful."

"Yeah. So it's probably best that you stay away. I wouldn't want you to get it, too."

Mum falls silent.

Has she been cut off?

"Mum," I say. "Are you still there?"

She finally speaks. "Is this about your father?"

"What do you mean?"

"Is this about what I asked you to get for me? Are you trying to avoid me?"

"No, Mum, of course not. We really are sick. Thea's off school today. She's still in bed."

"What's happening about the blood?"

"*Shush*, Mum. Don't even mention it, especially over the phone."

"How else am I supposed to ask you? You don't reply to any of my messages."

"I'm sorry. I've just been preoccupied."

"Sarah, your father hasn't got long left, so I need an answer: yes or no? It's not hard."

What the hell do I tell her? She's going to want the money back.

"Come on, Sarah," Mum pushes, "spit it out."

"Kate couldn't get it," I blurt out. "Her dealer's in prison."

"You're kidding me?"

"No, he's gone down for twenty years," I stutter, nervously. I can't help it. "They caught him with a houseful of drugs."

"Well, when did this happen?" she asks. *She knows I'm lying—I can sense it.*

"The other day." I'm drowning in lies. I need to end this conversation now. "Look, I told you it's dangerous to discuss this over the phone, so just change the subject. It's not happening, Mum."

"Okay then," she replies, suspiciously, "I'll get it from somewhere else. I'll pop round in a bit to get the money off you."

Shit! The five grand!

And then something occurs to me: I should have just given her *my blood* in a vial. She would have given it to Dad, realised it was fake, and be none the wiser.

Bloody hell! You're an idiot, Sarah!

"It's not safe to come here," I say, struggling to contain the alarm in my voice. "You'll catch the bug and give it to Dad. It's too risky."

"Don't pretend you give a shit about your father, Sarah. You're not fooling anyone."

"I care about you, though."

Through the phone, I can hear Mum sigh in frustration. "Do you have my money?"

I don't have an answer. I'm out of lies.

"Come on, Sarah," Mum says, "Where is it?"

What the hell do I say?

And then the words "I spent it," fall from my mouth.

"What! Already?" Mum screams down the phone. "On what?"

"I had to pay off a credit-card bill," I lie. *Where did that come from?* But every lie that passes my lips creates a whole new set of questions.

"You stupid girl, Sarah!" Mum snaps. "That money was for your father. How could you be so bloody selfish?"

"I'm sorry," I reply quietly, my finger hovering over the cancel button on the phone.

"*Sorry? Sorry?* You do realise that you've just *killed* your father. Are you happy now?"

Any other day, after any other of Mum's rants, I'd be consumed with guilt. But I have a daughter to take care of, and a body to bury. "I'll get you the money," I say, this time with authority. "But right now Thea is my priority. So I'm going, Mum. And I'm sorry."

"Well, that's just—" Mum starts to say, but I end the phone call mid-sentence.

I've got bigger problems—like how on earth am I going to get Jared to the garden? He's got to weigh at least ten stone. I need to put him into something like a body bag, that way I can drag him out. But what can I use instead of a body bag? Bin bags are too weak. I could go shopping for something, but I've already burned up way too much sunlight. There must be something in the house I can use.

A vile image of me hacking his body to pieces pops into my head. *Don't even think about it, Sarah. It's not going to happen.*

Just as I shake the thought away, the solution suddenly comes to me.

Mark's old sleeping bag!

I march into the hallway, stopping at the cupboard under the stairs. As soon as I open it I see a bloated bin bag filled with Mark's leftover junk. On my hands and knees, I scramble to drag it out, pushing past a bag of old coats I've been meaning to give to charity, a box of rusty tools that have never been used, and various other pieces of crap that have found their way in here. I rip the bag open, and the red and green sleeping bag with orange lining pops out like a Jack-in-the-box. I cough when a cloud of dust hits my face. The sleeping bag stinks of mildew, like a derelict old house. Not that it matters one bit. I ball it up and start to climb out of the cupboard, but then something catches my eye: Thea and Ivy's old baby monitor, still up on the shelf. Forgot I still had it. Picking it up, I peer down at the tiny, dusty screen. I wonder if it still works. I push the *On* button, but nothing happens. It probably just needs a charge. Why on earth did I keep this thing? Did I really think that I'd be having another child in the future? But when I pick up the camera from the shelf, all those memories of watching my little babies sleep come flooding back.

Some things are just too hard to part with.

If I can get it working again, I can use this monitor to watch over Thea. So I take it into the living room and plug it into the socket. The red charge light comes on, putting a tiny smile on my face. But then I remember what the sleeping bag is for, and realise that there's absolutely nothing to smile about.

I exit the living room and head up to Thea's room. At her door, I brace again, nerves creeping over me. What if Thea's wide-awake? Waiting for me?

No, I would have heard something by now.

Jesus Christ, I'm really afraid of my own daughter.

I take a slow, deep breath, and then unlock the door. Thea's weight is still pressing against it. It means she's still sleeping. *That's good.* I push hard on the door and then slip through the gap.

Inside, I can plainly see that Thea hasn't moved a muscle since earlier. *Please be breathing.* The panic dwindles when I see her chest moving. *Thank God.*

I walk over to Jared, stare down at his body, and hold back a rush of vomit. The carpet all around him is now a dark, reddish brown, and thick, almost as if he's lying on a rug. I doubt that will ever come clean again.

I pull the zip of the sleeping bag until it opens out completely, and then I lay it flat on the carpet beside him.

Now comes the part that I've been dreading. I let out a long exhalation and kneel down by his side. *Don't look at his face.* I slip my hands under his back and legs, and start to roll him onto the sleeping bag. His body feels stiff as if moving a piece of furniture. By accident, I catch a glimpse of his face; his eyes are closed, but his mouth is hanging wide open. *So is his throat*. I gag, and then swallow a little sick—but I keep focused, keep pushing until Jared's body is on the sleeping bag.

I zip him up all the way, with just his head sticking out of the top, and then grab two handfuls of sleeping bag. The fabric is puffy, so I have a decent grip. I lift him so that his blood-drenched head and shoulders are off the floor; I can't risk leaving a trail of it on the carpet. Just as I start to haul the body through the doorway, I realise something: I should've put him into the sleeping bag headfirst. *Bloody hell!*

I'll have to start again.

No, it's too late now. Keep moving.

On the landing, I stop when I see a trail of blood. "Shit!" *There's a fucking leak?* I quickly grab a towel from my bedroom and wipe down the sleeping bag. I can't see any obvious tears in the fabric. I must have just dragged it through the blood and gore on Thea's carpet. *Fucking hell!*

When I reach the top of the stairs, I pause for a moment. *How am I supposed to get him down? Roll him?* No, I'll just have to slide him, one step at a time. I start to lower the sleeping bag down carefully, feet first, struggling against his weight. When he reaches the centre of the staircase, my fingers start to slip, and I lose my hold. "*Oh fuck!*" I say as the body thuds against each step, the sound echoing around the house. Chasing after it, I almost lose my footing, so I grab hold of the banister. Jared's arm dangles out of the sleeping bag when he finally crashes onto the hallway floor. Wincing, I stuff it back inside and start to drag him along the hallway towards the back door, followed by another trail of blood.

In the kitchen, I stare at the blood for a moment. *What a mess.* I sigh and then rub away the beads of sweat from my brow. *It's fine, Sarah. Don't panic.* It should wipe off the wooden floor and kitchen tiles easily. And the carpets can be shampooed. It's just like red wine.

Lots of red wine.

21

The ground is tough, forcing me to hit the dead grass as hard as I can. And each time I do, I check if the neighbours are watching. Luckily, the wall is a little too high on the left side of the garden, but Mary's fence on the right side is only about five feet high, with a thin gap between each wooden slat. In my mind, I see her head popping over, peering down at me, wondering why on earth I'm digging a great big hole in the garden. I suppose I could make up some bullshit story about re-turfing the lawn, especially given the state it's in. But what happens if the police come calling? What if they ask Mary if she's seen anything suspicious?

Digging a human-sized hole in your garden isn't exactly inconspicuous.

Maybe an hour and a half passes before it's deep

enough to fit the body. Another foot or so down would be better, but I need to get rid of the evidence now. The sun will be down in a few hours, and Thea will be up—confused and hungry. I need to be up there, ready to keep her calm.

Calm?

How the hell am I meant to do that? Watch a movie? Sing her a lullaby? She's a vampire, for Christ's sake! There's no calming her down! She can't be reasoned with. Not right now anyway. The only thing that will calm her down is time.

And blood.

Back aching, arms and legs fatigued, I drag the sleeping bag out of the kitchen, along the garden, and then roll it into the hole. It lands with a loud thump, causing me to scan for witnesses again. It's about three feet deep, six feet in length, and around two feet wide. Using the spade, I prod the sleeping bag until it fits snugly into the hole, all the while refusing to look at Jared's face.

I quickly shovel the dirt back down into the hole until the body is completely submerged. On my knees, I scoop up handfuls of dirt and scatter it across the lawn. Once that's done, I finish by flattening out the mound with the back of the spade. There's a rusty old wheelbarrow by the shed, left here from the previous owner. I wheel it over to the centre of the heap, concealing the evidence.

I try not to think that there's a boy buried in my garden. But it's impossible. I see Thea again, crouched over him, his throat torn out, blood gushing all over everything. I see his face, lifeless and—

Shut up, Sarah!

This was just a nasty mess that needed to be cleaned up! Jared isn't worth crying over! The little bastard was going to take Thea away from me!

After everything I've been through!

What kind of monster would do that to a mother?

I take another look around and then head for the house.

What about *his* mother? And his father? They'll be wondering where the hell their son is. They'll be crushed when they find out. *Suicidal.* Like I was.

Reaching the back door, I glance at the grave, imagining police exhuming the body, Jared's parents falling to their knees at the sight of their rotting son. My hands start to quake, and I'm suddenly short of breath. *I think I'm going to faint.* I squeeze the door-frame as hard as I can, but my body slides down until I'm on my knees.

I see an image Thea's face—*before I poisoned her* —and I focus on it.

That's what I'm fighting for. *My angel.* All this guilt, this self-pity will have to be put on hold. Thea is still sick, and she's not likely to get better any time soon. So once she is, once she can control her urges, then we'll leave this house. For good. Let the police come for us. Let them unearth the body. By then we'll be long gone, away from boys, away from Mum and that *tosser* of a father. We'll start a new life, with a new home. Thea won't need friends—or school. She'll have me to look out for her, to teach her. The way it should have been from the start.

My hands start to settle; so does my breathing. I straighten up, the faint feeling gone, and enter the house.

Time to get cleaning.

22

Thea is sleeping on her bed. I gaze up at her every few seconds as I scrub the blood from her carpet. Even though she looks like the same sweet Thea, seeing her wrists and ankles tied to the metal bedframe turns my stomach more than Jared's blood ever could.

The mess on the walls and wardrobe wiped off pretty easily, but the carpet stain is deep, so I've had to use every cleaning product I could find in the house. Some of it is coming up, but not enough to hide the evidence if someone came snooping. And I can't exactly say that the stain is just red wine—the area is just too big. You'd need a crate of it to make that excuse convincing.

After more than two hours spent on my hands and knees, I finally stand up and inspect the job. The carpet is ruined, so I drag Thea's white, fluffy rug directly over the stain. It's not the ideal solution, but it'll have to do for now.

I sit on the edge of the bed, staring at the thin rope around Thea's wrists. I hope I didn't tie them too tight. I wouldn't want to cut off the circulation. What if I end up permanently damaging her hands?

She's a vampire. She'll heal.

But I had to restrain her, at least for the time being. She's a long way off from controlling her urges. *So be patient*—ride it out until the end of the week and see what happens.

I still haven't told the school. They'll be calling tomorrow, asking where she is. I'd better phone them first thing, tell them she has a bug. The last thing I need right now is Social Services pestering me.

I notice the clock on the bedside cabinet. 5:12 P.M. It'll be dark in a couple of hours. I feel nauseated just thinking about Thea the way she was last night. Like a wild animal tearing into its prey. It was horrendous! Maybe tonight will be better. Who knows what difference twenty-four hours will make?

At her bedside, I check that the ropes are tight enough, and then kiss her on her cheek. It feels cold.

Too cold.

I try to put the worry to the back of my mind. There'll be plenty of time for that when the sun disappears.

I walk over to the doorway, blow her a kiss, and then lock Thea in.

Outside her room, I press my back against the wall and close my eyes. Jared's distorted face still haunts me; can't seem to shake it off.

A big *fucking* drink should do the trick.

I'm sitting at the kitchen table, finishing off a ham and cheese sandwich. I'm not in the least bit hungry, but I haven't eaten a thing all day. How could I though, after what I had to do?

I stare at the sky through the window. It's now a dark orange as the sun begins to set.

Not long now. Any minute.

I should be upstairs, getting ready for Thea to wake, but I can't seem to move. I know I'm just delaying the inevitable. I know I should be up there, by her side, but my body is glued to the chair.

I force the last piece of sandwich into my mouth, and then wash it down my throat with the red wine. It's not the best of flavour combinations, but right now, right before I have to face Thea, my cuisine is the last of my priorities.

Should I make something else to eat? Fry up some chicken for later? No, I should give the hallway and tiles another mop. The police might find something I've missed. I've watched enough *CSI* to know how difficult it is to get rid of evidence.

Don't be such a coward, Sarah! You know what you're doing. Staying down here won't take away the problem. You have to face up to what you've done and deal with it. Head on!

Of course I'm going to face up to it. That's my daughter up there. I just need a few more minutes to prepare myself.

Finishing what's left of my glass, I grab the bottle and start to fill it back up. Before it's even halfway full, I hear a loud cry coming from upstairs.

She's awake.

My heart sinks; my stomach fills with butterflies. *It's time.* I get up off the chair, and my legs turn to jelly. I let out a long sigh and then gulp down the wine in one go.

Don't be afraid.

I walk over to the cupboard, reach far into the back and pull out Thea's plastic cup. It's covered in dust, so I blow on it hard. She hasn't used this for nearly ten years. Couldn't bring myself to throw it out. Over by the microwave, I pull out a small knife from the wooden rack, and then a pack of alcohol-wipes from the medicine cupboard. I carry the items out of the kitchen and up the stairs. Each step seems larger than the one before. My vision is narrowing; my knees feel weak.

The screams are getting louder.

On the landing, I grab hold of the banister to steady myself.

What's wrong with me? She's my daughter. She needs me.

I take a deep breath and then continue forward to her door.

You can do this. It's just Thea.

She's not a monster.

I take another breath, unlock the door, and then slowly open it.

The moment I step inside, Thea looks at me. I shudder when I see her face; so pale and distorted, creased up with rage, the veins in her neck pulsating as she shrieks and tugs violently at the restraints.

Body shaking, I somehow managed a fake smile. "Don't worry, sweetheart," I stammer, "Mummy's here. Everything's going to be all right."

Don't panic. You can do this, Sarah. She's your daughter.

Walking over to the desk, positioned on the other side of her bed, I watch Thea as her eyes and head follow my every footstep; her cries turning into snake-like hisses, coming from between her clenched teeth. I set the plastic cup down on the desk and lay my left hand on my knee, palm facing upwards.

"Everything's going to be okay, angel," I reassure her, rolling my cardigan sleeve up to my elbow. "Mummy will fix it. I promise." I rub the alcohol-wipe over my arm and knife, "And we can put this great big mess behind us," and then stick the blade into the outside of my forearm. Avoiding any veins, I start to reopen an old scar. Wincing, I stop when I've sliced about an inch or two of flesh. Blood begins to leak out from the wound, running down my arm, pooling in my hand. I drop the knife down on the desk, and quickly hang my dripping arm over the cup.

Be strong. This is nothing compared to burying a body in your garden. Nothing compared to losing Ivy. Remember that.

Thea sees my oozing arm and the hissing suddenly stops. Her eyes light up as she watches the cup slowly fill up with blood. I keep tensing my arm, clenching my fist until I start to feel queasy.

This is bugger all blood. It's barely fifty mills. You've given blood lots of times. Stop your whining, woman!

After a few minutes, Thea starts to hiss again, which quickly turns into a deafening squeal.

She's tired of waiting.

Reaching over to my left, I open the bottom drawer of Thea's chest and pull out a white vest. I wrap it around my bleeding forearm and tie it tightly.

"Are you hungry, sweetheart?" I ask her as I carry the cup over to the bed. I manage to steady my hand as I move the cup towards Thea's mouth. "Is this what you want?" She starts to thrash, forcing me to move the cup away. I can't spill a drop. "Calm down, honey." With one hand pressing her chest down, I hold her body onto the bed. I hover the cup under her chin and slowly pour the blood into her mouth. The first few drops just hit her teeth and lips, dripping down her chin and neck. But then she licks her lips, opens her mouth, and lets me empty the entire contents in. I quickly move off the bed, watching her as she gulps it down like Coke.

But is it enough to hold her? She drank Jared dry

yesterday—and she was still aggressive. Maybe I need to cut my other forearm.

Just wait, Sarah. See what happens.

I sit back down on the chair, keeping the pressure on my bleeding arm, and watch her as she pulls on the ropes, barking at me. Why can't she say something? "Come on, honey. It's Mummy. Speak to me."

My chin starts to quiver as I try to find my daughter, hidden behind the rage. "I know you're in there, Thea. You just need a little time. That's all."

Don't cry, Sarah. You have to be strong.

I shake off the tears and pull out one of Thea's books from her shelf. It's my old Ladybird book of *Three Billy Goats Gruff*. Some of the pages have been defaced by pen, and the spine is broken, but it still does the job. The troll was terrifying; it gave me nightmares up until I was eight. And for that reason, I hung on to the bloody thing. And this is why Thea wanted it. She found it fascinating that a book could have such an effect on me. The troll didn't scare her, or Ivy—in fact, they both found it hilarious that it kept me awake at night.

But as I stare at the face of the troll, and even though it takes me back to those nightmares, I see now the significance. It was just a story, just a painting. It wasn't real. And only real-life should be scary. Only losing your family should give you nightmares.

"Do you remember this book, Thea?" I say to her softly, showing her the cover. She looks at it. I think she recognises it. "The Three Billy Goats Gruff."

Thea snaps her blood-soaked teeth in my direction. I try not to let it bother me. It'll pass. I have faith.

I open the page and start to read, as if Thea were four again, lying on her bed, hanging on my every word, looking forward to hearing what silly voice I would do this time.

I'll finish this book, and then I'll read another— and another until the sun comes up. And I'll do exactly the same thing tomorrow night, and the next, and the one after that—until this nightmare is well and truly over.

And I get my little girl back safely.

23

Today is going to be a good day—I'm feeling very optimistic.

Unfortunately you can't get needles and syringes over the counter, so I've ordered some from the Internet. Next day delivery. Can't keep slicing my arm every time Thea gets hungry. I'll get animal blood eventually, when things settle down. Maybe lamb or beef. But right now I've got too much on my plate even to venture outside the house.

I've also called the school, told them that Thea has a bug and won't be in for the rest of the week. I called mum to apologise and said that she'd get her money in the next few weeks. The conversation didn't exactly go well, but it's a start. At least she didn't call me a murderer this time.

I'll take *bitch* over murderer any day of the week.

But the best news of all is Thea. The thrashing started to cease at around four in the morning. Maybe it takes a few hours for the blood to take effect. But without a doubt, she was calmer than she was that first night. Just got to keep feeding her, and with a bit of luck, I can untie those awful restraints.

It's 3:51 P.M. I managed to get a few hours sleep this morning, just after Thea passed out. This is nothing to me. I've lived a vampire's routine for years working the night shift. It was hard at first, but it doesn't take long to get used to it.

Once I finish my bowl of tomato and basil soup, I soak up what's left with the last of the bread, and then do the dishes. There's still some dried up vomit in the sink from the other day. I forgot all about it.

I'm almost looking forward to Thea waking. It'll be good to compare each night to the last. God, maybe she'll start talking to me. Who knows!

Don't get ahead of yourself, Sarah. One step at a time.

I finish up in the kitchen, pour myself a well-deserved glass of red, and then take it into the living room. *Time to relax, I think.* I sit on the couch and put on the TV. There's a *Friends* marathon showing. I've seen every episode countless times—but who the hell cares? It's bloody great! Sipping my wine, I notice the baby-monitor on the coffee table. I'm surprised how well it still works. The picture isn't perfect, but it gives me a decent view of Thea from the camera as she sleeps. Just like old times.

This is one of my favourite episodes. It's the one where Ross buys leather trousers and they shrink. I know exactly when the jokes are coming, but I still can't help but laugh.

It feels good to laugh again.

And by this weekend, I'll be sitting down on this couch, curled up with Thea, watching a movie.

The doorbell rings.

I suddenly jump up in fright, almost knocking my empty glass off the coffee table.

Shit! I must have dozed off.

The room is much darker now. Heart soaring, I check my watch. 7:25 P.M.

"Shit!"

I check the baby-monitor.

Thea's still asleep. *Thank God!*

The doorbell goes off again

Who the hell is that?

Mum?

Oh shit, I bet it's Kate! I was supposed to work last

night. I forgot to bloody call in sick.

Bugger!

It rings for a third time as I exit the living room, heading for the front door. Should I pretend I'm not home? If it's Mum, she'll want to see Thea—even if she thinks she has a bug. Maybe it's the neighbour, asking about all those screams from last night.

I better answer it. I don't want to arouse any suspicion.

I take a deep breath, try to slow my pulse rate, and then open it with a big forced grin.

Standing in the doorway is a woman, mid-twenties with blonde hair tied back in a ponytail. Next to her a tall man in his late-thirties.

I start to feel dizzy.

It's the police.

"Mrs Wilkes?" the male police officer asks.

"Yes," I reply, frowning as if I have absolutely no clue why they're here. "Is everything all right?"

"There's nothing to worry about," he replies. "I'm Officer Davies, and this is my colleague, Officer Lewis. We've had a report of a missing person. Do you mind if we come in for a quick chat?"

I think I'm going to throw up.

"Now's not a good time," I reply. "I've got a terrible bug. I don't want to pass it on to you." *They know I'm lying. I can feel their judging eyes burning into me. I bet they'll ask me where I buried the body.*

"I'm sorry to hear that, Mrs Wilkes," the female says with a sympathetic tone. "We promise we won't keep you too long."

I'll have to let them in—otherwise it's obvious that I'm hiding something.

"*Urrr...*yes, all right then," I say, moving back to give them room. "Just don't get too close to me."

The officers smile as they enter the house. I usher them quickly along the hallway, terrified that I might have missed a speck of blood.

Switching on the light, they follow me into the living room, and I point them towards the couch. "Please—take a seat."

"Thank you, Mrs Wilkes," the female officer says as they sit down.

"Can I get you anything?" I ask, faking polite smile—*which I'm positive they can see through.* "Tea? Coffee?" I spot my empty wine glass on the coffee table. "Wine?" I ask playfully. But then my smile vanishes when I notice the baby-monitor.

Oh shit!

Did they see it? They must know that I don't have a baby in the house.

Or do they?

Of course they bloody know! They're police! They know everything!

Calm down, Sarah. You can do this.

"We're fine, thank you," the male officer replies. "We just need to ask you a few questions about a missing boy."

"Of course," I say, clenching my fists tightly to stop them from shaking. "Which boy?"

"Jared Thomas?" the male officer says. "I've spoken to his mother, and she believes that he was in a relationship with your daughter: Thea Wilkes."

I take a seat on the armchair, shaking my head in protest. "Unfortunately, my daughter and I haven't been getting on so well lately. So there's very little she tells me. She just comes home, grunts at me, and puts her head in that bloody iPad of hers. Spends all evening chatting with her friends."

"Oh right, I see," the female officer says. "May we speak to Thea? Ask her a few questions? Maybe Jared mentioned to her where he was planning on going. Would that be all right, Mrs Wilkes?"

I feel sick. The room is shrinking. I have a body in the garden, a blood-stained carpet—and a vampire tied to the bed.

"Just a quick chat," the male officer says. "I'm sure there's nothing to worry about, but the first forty-eight hours are crucial, so any help whatsoever would be very much appreciated."

They can sense my reluctance. They can see it a mile off.

I look at the window—the sun is just minutes away from setting. "It's not a good time at the moment," I say, cagily. "Thea has the same bug as I have. She's a little worse though. She's actually in bed right now, so I'd rather not disturb her—if that's okay. She didn't get a wink of sleep last night." *Shut up, Sarah. You're waffling on.* "But I'll speak to her about it—*first thing.* I promise."

"It's fine, Mrs Wilkes," the female officer says with a smile. "Let her get some rest and ask her when she's feeling better."

"Thank you," I say. "I wish I could have been more helpful. And I hope you find the boy."

"I'm sure we will, Mrs Wilkes," the female officer says as she gets up off the couch. The male officer follows her up.

The sun has almost vanished. They need to leave right now.

I open the living-room door to usher them out. Just as I do, a faint crackle comes out of the baby-monitor.

Thea's awake!

The male officer glances down at the device just as it makes another sputtering. "What's that?" he asks.

Putting on my best impersonation of a calm woman, I pick it up, hiding the screen with my hand. "Oh, it's just Thea's old baby-monitor," I say, discreetly switching it off. "She was sick a few times yesterday—couldn't keep a thing down—so I was worried that she might choke in her sleep. I'm paranoid about things like that. Especially after losing my eldest daughter."

"Oh, I'm sorry to hear that," the female officer says, pursing her lips. "We'll get out of your hair now. Thank you again, Mrs Wilkes. And let us know if Thea can tell us anything about Jared's whereabouts."

"No problem at all," I say, steering them into the hallway, towards the front door. My muscles clench when we pass the stairs. All it would take is one scream from Thea, and the game would be up.

I should have gagged her.

I open the door, and the officers step outside.

"Thanks again, Mrs Wilkes," the male officer says. "We'll be in touch."

Just as I start to close the door, there's a weak scream from upstairs.

Shit! Did they hear it?

There's another one as the door clicks shut. *This time much louder.*

They definitely heard that one!

Oh shit!

I peek through the spy hole in the centre of the door. *They're on to me. They're probably calling for back-up right now.*

I see the officers; they're walking over to their police car. It's too hard to tell for sure if they heard. They haven't looked back at the house yet. If they did hear a scream, wouldn't they be bursting through the front door right this second?

They could be scoping me out, seeing how I'd react to a visit from the police.

"Shit! Shit! Shit!"

I race upstairs, into Thea's bedroom. She growls at me the moment she sees me. She's hungry.

"Hi, sweetheart," I say with clenched teeth, trying to undo the thick knot in my stomach. "How are you feeling tonight? Any better?"

She doesn't answer me. But at least she's not screaming. That's progress.

I go over to the desk chair again and sit. I feel exhausted; nerves still unsettled. The thought of someone taking away my little girl drives a stake through my heart. I wipe the beads of sweat from my forehead and then turn to Thea. "Are you hungry, angel? I bet you are."

She hisses. It almost sounds like 'Yes'.

A glimmer of hope?

It puts a genuine smile on my face as I roll my sleeve up and rub my arm and knife with the alcohol-wipe. Just as I place the blade against my forearm, about to reopen the cut, I hear a car engine start from outside. Hurrying over to the window, I peek through the curtains. I see the police car pulling off down the street. *They took their time leaving.*

They *were* watching me!

This is bad. This is very bad.

"We've got to leave this house, Thea." I sit back down on the chair and start to cut my forearm. This time, I don't feel the pain. "It has to be tonight. The police will be back, and they'll try to take you away from me." I start to drain the blood into the cup. There's less this time. "But I won't let them. I'd rather *die* than lose you."

I climb onto the bed and carefully pour the blood into Thea's open mouth. She doesn't try to squirm or buck. She's so much calmer than yesterday. Another day or two and she'll be back to her old self.

I can celebrate later—right now I've got to pack.

I sprint over to the wardrobe and pull down Thea's pink suitcase from the top. It's covered in dust; she hasn't used this in years. I start to fill it.

Thea's eyes follow me around the room. They shouldn't disturb me—but they do.

Not long now. Just a few more days.

Once the suitcase is full to the brim with clothes, shoes, underwear, a few random CDs, her iPad, and a few other knickknacks, I drag it out onto the landing and dash into my bedroom. I pull down the big black suitcase from the top shelf of my wardrobe and open it. It still has small miniature toiletries left over from our last holiday. Within a matter of minutes, I've managed to fill the case to bursting point with clothes, shoes, makeup and a few books. The rest isn't important. I lug it out onto the landing and set it down by Thea's.

Next stop: *the kitchen.*

Just as I make my way towards the staircase, I freeze outside Ivy's room. I walk in, staring at all the memories that I'll be leaving behind.

I can't just abandon all these things.

But I have to. I can't stay. The police will come. They'll find the bloodstain; they'll see the freshly dug mound of dirt in the garden.

Maybe I'll just take a few things with me as a reminder. I grab the framed photos, her sketchbook, a few soft toys she managed to hang onto, and the painting of Thea from the wall.

That'll have to do. I don't need possessions to remember her. Everything that was wonderful about her is forever etched onto my soul.

I swallow hard and then blow the room a kiss.

I shake off the anguish, and then place Ivy's suitcase on the landing next to the others.

I head down onto the hallway. There's a cupboard directly under the staircase. I open it. Inside, I pull out a large sports bag. It's filled with old shoes and handbags. God knows why. I must have put them there to take to the charity shop. I empty them out and carry the bag into the kitchen. I can't leave the house without food, so I practically throw in the entire contents of the fridge, the cereal cupboards, and whatever biscuits and crisps are left in the kitchen. I spot the last bottle of red on the worktop. I think about putting it in the bag, but instead, I grab the corkscrew, open it, and take a giant swig straight from the bottle. I'm past caring about social etiquette.

I need money.

All I find inside my purse is a twenty-pound note, about five pounds in loose change, and a credit card. My hand starts to shake again as I place the purse on the table. I suddenly feel giddy, so I sit down on the chair.

What the hell am I doing?

I've got no money. Nowhere to go. And I can't use my credit card because the police will trace it. And even if I did have money and a place to go, I can't even think about moving Thea until the sun comes up. She's not ready.

Think, Sarah! Think!

I need help.

Kate?

No, I can't drag her into this. She's already done enough for me.

Mum?

No, I'd have to be *mad* to tell her what I did.

But she's the only one that I can trust. And she has money.

I've got to. There's no one else. I can't do this alone.

Gulping down the wine, not stopping for air, I

think about Mum's reaction if I told her what I did to Thea.

She'd hate me.

Detest me.

She'll disown me.

I take another huge swig and then take the bottle into the living room. At the window, I peek outside onto the street. I don't see any police cars. But there will be. It's just a matter of time. I hope to God they hold off until tomorrow. What on earth would I do if they came before dawn?

They'd take everything from me. In a matter of moments.

I finish the bottle, wiping the residue from my lips.

That's it—I'm out of options. I'll have to tell Mum.

But what the hell do I say? That I infected my own daughter? That there's a teenage boy buried in my garden?

No.

I could tell her that Thea just found the blood in my sock drawer. Maybe she thought it was something else.

No, I can't. Mum would never forgive herself. I'll just need to tell her that I'm desperate for money.

Maybe a secret gambling debt. Yeah, that might work. First thing in the morning, I'll take out as much cash from the ATM as I can, and then stop off at Mum's house to grab some money. She doesn't have to know the truth; she's got enough on her plate with Dad. Thea and I will head down to South Wales; find some cheap place to rent. Hell, maybe Kate's got a few connections for a job—off the books of course.

Yeah, I can do this. *We* can do this. People run away all the time.

I take a slow, deep breath, and then pick up the house-phone from its cradle. My heart races when I dial Mum's number.

I'm starting to regret this already. Should I hang up?

No, Sarah—you need money.

The phone keeps ringing.

It goes to voicemail.

Where the hell is she? In the shower? Sleeping?

I ring again.

Voicemail again.

I dial her mobile phone instead.

"Hi, Sarah," Mum answers, her voice croaky.

"Hi, Mum. You sound hoarse," I say. "Is every-thing all right?"

She doesn't answer.

"*Mum*," I say, "what's wrong?"

I hear the sound of weeping.

"Your father's passed away," Mum snivels.

That sentence should be meaningless to me, especially after the life that that man gave me, and especially in the light of everything Thea is going through. But for some reason, a reason that makes absolutely no sense at all, I burst into tears.

Why?

For Mum?

I move the phone away from my face as I wait for the sobbing to pass. When it finally does, I hear the faint sound of Mum calling my name, so I return the phone to my ear.

"Are you okay?" she asks.

I sniff loudly, wiping the tears from my eyes. "I'm fine. I'm just in shock, that's all." *Shock? There's no shock. The man was days away from dying. The only shock is feeling these tears running down my cheeks.*

"I'm still at the hospital with Uncle Roy," Mum says. "Do you and Thea want to come down?"

"We can't leave the house. Thea's too sick."

"That's okay, Sarah. I'll be leaving here soon. Is it all right if I come up to your house? I don't think I can go back home alone tonight."

A rush of panic shunts me.

She can't come here tonight. Not with Thea so ill? It's too much. Neither of us is in a fit state to cope.

But maybe it's better that way. She can see the mess for herself. She'll understand. *She'll have to.* She's already lost a husband and a granddaughter. She knows what will happen to Thea and I if the police find us. She's not an idiot.

Yes. Face to face is better.

"Of course you can, Mum," I reply. No turning back now. It's done.

I sigh, my mouth away from the phone. It's the right thing to do. A moment in Thea's room and she'll see how desperate I am.

"Thank you," Mum says. "I'll see you soon."

"Okay. I love you."

"I love you, too, Sarah."

I press the cancel button on the phone and then return it to its cradle.

Mum should come with us. There's nothing left to stay for. And she knows lots of people. All over. She's bound to have somewhere for us to lay low.

Suddenly the room starts to spin, the effects of the wine hitting me hard. Closing my eyes, I sit back on the couch, my body sinking into the cushions, and wait for the feeling to pass.

After a few minutes of silence, I open my eyes. The fog has lifted, but the chaos all around me is still here.

The baby monitor on the coffee table catches my eye. Pushing the *On* button, I stare at the small screen as it lights up, coming to life.

I see Thea's bed—*it's empty.*

My heart stops dead as I drop the monitor. It hits the floor with a crack.

"*Oh, shit!*"

Racing out of the living room, bolting up the staircase, all that's coursing through my mind is Thea loose on the streets, all alone. I leap over the suitcases and then take out the skeleton key from my pocket. My entire body tightens up in panic when I see that Thea's door is wide open.

Jesus Christ, I forgot to lock it!

Bursting in, I find her bed still empty and the ropes scattered across the quilt. *Oh, fuck. Where've you got to, Thea?* Scanning the room, I don't see her anywhere.

"Thea?" I call out softly, disguising the fear in my voice. "Where are you, sweetheart?"

I listen out for movement; maybe she's hiding. I dart over to the window. It's still locked. Opening the wardrobe, I separate the hanging clothes at the centre. She's not there.

"Thea," I call out again, this time a little louder. "Mummy needs to speak to you."

Nothing.

I bet she's hiding under the bed.

Throat dry with trepidation, I drop to one knee. "Thea, don't be afraid," I say as I lift the quilt to see under the bed. "Mummy's not going to hurt you."

It's deserted. Just a few stray shoes, old magazines and other bits of junk. *Where the hell is she?*

"Thea?"

Just as I begin to stand, I hear something. It's the sound of shallow breathing.

It's coming from above me.

"Mum," a gravelly, strained voice says. "I'm here."

I slowly move my eyes up to the ceiling—*and then gasp in horror*. Thea is staring down at me, clutching the light-fitting with both hands and bare feet.

I try to speak, to call her name, but no words form. I slowly reach up to her, staring at her inflamed eyes, her wide mouth, oozing with brown spit.

Just as my fingers are within inches of her, she suddenly drops down, crashing onto my body.

I shriek in fright as she pins me to the floor, her hands pressing down hard on my wrists.

"Thea!" I yell, wriggling and squirming, trying desperately to throw her off me. "Stop it!"

She doesn't hear me as she aims her mouth at my neck. Managing to move my head a little, her teeth miss, sinking into the top of my right shoulder instead. The pain is unbearable as her jaw clamps down, cutting through my skin. I shrug my shoulder violently, dislodging her mouth, and then buck my hips as hard as I can. Thea's body flies off me, her back crashing against the bed. I pull my wrists free from her iron grip and scramble to my feet, running towards the doorway. With no time to close the door after me, Thea chases me out onto the landing. Blood pouring from my shoulder, my vision narrowing from the pain, I sprint towards the stairs.

This is not my daughter!

This is not Thea!

I leap over the suitcases again, but this time my foot clips a handle. In a swirl of colours, I fly head-first down the stairs. I try to grab the banister but my shoulder slams painfully into it. So does the side of my face. In a split second, I'm at the bottom, my back in agony, staring up at Thea as she scurries after me. Head throbbing, vision blurry, I crawl across the hallway towards the kitchen. My crawl turns into a sprint as the sound of Thea landing on the hallway hits my ears.

Hissing like a snake, she reaches me in no time, digging her nails into my forearm. I twist my body viciously, freeing myself from her grip.

Charging into the kitchen, I take the handle and slam the door into her face. My stomach somersaults when I hear the cracking sound of her nose.

Oh, Jesus Christ! Jesus Christ! I'm so sorry, angel.

The blow doesn't stop her. Instead, she thrusts the door, screaming like a psychopath. I tug at the handle with both hands. She's strong—*I can't hold it.*

"*Stop it, Thea!*" I cry. "*Please!*"

The snarls are deafening as the handle starts to slip from my grasp. Sweat pouring, I glance at the window. It's still dark outside. The sun is hours away. The handle is yanked from my hand, and the door is pulled open. With no other options, I make a dash for the back door. *Is it locked?* I grab the handle and the door opens. Rushing through the gap, I'm outside running along the concrete path, heading for the garden gate. There's a thick bolt-lock on the gate. It's always stiff, so I pull on it hard. After a second or two, the gate opens and I'm out onto the pavement, racing, heading to God-knows-where.

As I whizz past the houses, fences, and driveways, something dawns on me: *Thea isn't chasing me.*

Why?

Has she come to her senses? Seen the damage she's done?

I slow down, coming to a complete stop about a hundred metres from home. *She's scared. She's all alone in the house. Sick and disorientated. She needs help.* My *help.*

What kind of mother abandons their daughter in the middle of the night?

I start to run back towards the house. She's my little girl. *She's not a monster.* I prod my stinging shoulder, cringing in pain. *She doesn't know what she's doing. She can't help it.* At the garden gate, I wipe the blood on my jeans, take a deep breath, and then open it.

"Thea?" I whisper as I step into the dark garden, faintly lit by the moonlight. "Are you out here?" There's no response. "Thea? It's Mummy."

Pulse rising, I scan my surroundings, expecting her to jump out at any moment. But the garden is small; there aren't that many hiding places. She's still inside the house. Probably cowering under her bed.

Mummy's coming, sweetheart!

The back door is still hanging open. Cautiously

stepping into the kitchen, I try to push the dread to the back of my mind.

Don't be afraid, Sarah. It's just Thea.

The kitchen is deserted.

What if she's fled the house? She might hurt someone.

What if I never see her again?

Shut up, Sarah! She's here! This is her home, for Christ's sake! She's just gone back to her bedroom to calm down. That's all.

"Thea," I whisper as my entire body trembles. "It's Mummy."

The house is eerily silent as I step onto the hallway. "Thea?"

Nothing.

At the foot of the stairs, I peer up to the landing. I can't see her. "Thea?" I open the living-room door and slowly step inside; my body clenched, ready for an attack. Walking over to the couch, I glance behind it. She's not there. Why would she be there? This isn't a game. She's hungry. She wouldn't toy with me.

I exit the living room and make my way upstairs. What if she's hurt?

Or worse...

I check the bathroom; it's empty. Across the landing, I step over the suitcases as I reach Ivy's bedroom. The room is dark, with just the light from the landing seeping in. Poking my head inside, I shudder in fright when I see the bed. Thea is lying on her side, facing the window. *Ivy?* From here, she looks just like her sister. Like the last time I saw her.

Maybe it is her.

"Thea?" I whisper, sweat trickling down my face.

She hears my voice and slowly sits up. She turns to me, and I see Thea's tear-filled eyes, dried blood stuck to the sides of her mouth.

"I'll never run out on you again," I say as I walk towards the bed. "I should have been stronger. I thought I was." I sit on the bed as my eyes start to fill with tears. "But it's always been you, sweetheart. You've always been the strong one. Not me, or Ivy. Just you. You've been through so much, and you're still here, still with me." I reach for her hand. She looks at it for a moment, but then takes it. "I'm sorry for what I put you through. But I promise—*as God is my witness*—I will spend the rest of my days trying to put things right. Can you ever forgive me?"

My racing heart begins to slow as Thea smiles.

She's come home to me.

And I'll never let her down again.

But then I see her eyes slowly shifting downwards to my bleeding shoulder, and that wonderful smile disappears.

"What's wrong?" I ask as she starts to squeeze my hand. "You're hurting me, Thea."

Suddenly she lunges at me, pushing me off the bed.

"Stop it, Thea!" I cry as she pins me to the carpet, this time with even more force. I scream out in agony when she clamps her jaws around my neck. I twist and squirm, but she's locked on tight. I close my eyes in pain as her teeth pierce my skin.

No, Thea! Please!

I manage to free one of my hands, so I grab a handful of her hair, pulling as hard as I can. Thea cries out as her blood-drenched mouth comes away from my neck.

"Get off me, Thea!" I shout, still pulling on her hair. "You're hurting Mummy." But she grasps my wrist from her head and slams it back onto the floor.

"No, Thea!" I shriek as she drops her head onto my neck, her teeth re-piercing the skin; the pain coursing down my spine.

I hear the sound of swallowing as she sucks hard.

"Help me!"

Thea's head comes up, my blood running down from her lips onto her chin.

But it's only to catch a breath.

Her teeth clamp down again.

I start to feel lightheaded, weak. *But this is not how I plan to die. Not at the hands of my own daughter.* I somehow find the strength to push my hips high off the floor, lifting Thea's body up. Twisting frantically, I manage to free myself from her grip. Clambering on my hands and knees towards the doorway, I feel Thea's full weight land on top of my back. My face hits the carpet, cracking my front tooth. But I keep crawling, ignoring the agony in my mouth. She bites down on the side of my neck, tearing a fresh piece of skin clean off. But this time, there's no pain, no panic —just sadness.

But even when things get bad, there is always hope.

Thea will *get better. She* will *be mine again.*

I just have to stay alive.

In the distance, I hear the sound of the back door opening.

Mum!

I keep slithering towards the noise, towing Thea on my back, blood now pooling around my head.

I hear footsteps on the tiles of the kitchen floor.

"*Help me, Mum,*" I try to shout with strained, barely audible words. "*Please!*"

My vision starts to blur, the noise of slurping and

swallowing becomes a distant echo. I can barely keep my eyes open.

But I have to.

I have to live.

I hear feet trudging up the stairs.

Mum.

In the haze, I see a figure standing over me.

Mum?

Thea retracts her head from my neck. A gush of air hits my lungs as she dismounts me. I slowly turn my head around to see Thea standing next to someone. A woman.

But it's not Mum.

My eyes strain and the fog begins to lift. The woman is Kate.

She smiles at Thea and kneels down in front of her. My little girl returns a smile. With her fingers, Kate wipes some of the blood off Thea's lips.

"*Help me,*" I say, trying to reach for them.

Kate looks at me, licks her fingers, and then shakes her head.

"*What are you doing?*" I ask as she takes Thea's hand.

She doesn't reply as they start to walk away, heading for the stairs.

"*Come back! Where are you going?*"

Kate stops, turns her head and glares at me. "I'm sorry, Sarah. But she belongs to me now." She carries on down the stairs, disappearing out of sight. "You don't deserve her."

"What are you talking about? Come back here. She's not yours."

The fog returns, but much thicker. I fight hard to keep my eyes open, but I end up losing.

I see Thea and Ivy playing outside in the garden. The mound of dirt above Jared's rotting body has gone. In my head, there is no death, no sadness. Just my two angels.

The images begin to fade. The light of my family disappearing.

I try to hang onto it, but the darkness takes hold, and I'm left with nothing.

And the last sound I remember is the back door slamming.

Also Available

Thea II:
A Vampire Story

Teenage life. Miles from home. And a taste for human blood.

Struggling to control her newfound bloodlust, Thea is taken to a secluded farmhouse by Kate, an experienced vampire with a dark past.

In the shadows, far from watchful eyes, a young life will begin to transform and leave behind the little girl she once knew.

For now, Thea is safe with Kate: her teacher, her friend, her protector.

But is this woman really all that she seems?

Available at: www.steven-jenkins.com

FREE BOOKS

For a limited time, you can download FREE copies of *Spine, Burn The Dead*: *Book 1 & Book 2* - The No.1 bestsellers from Steven Jenkins.

Available at: www.steven-jenkins.com

Also Available

Blue Skin: Book One

What will you do when they come for your children?

The world has turned inward, away from the sun, in the wake of a mysterious disease that has altered the human race. No longer able to bear human children, our mothers and daughters have brought vampire-like hybrids into the world, and with it a new order. Now that reproduction has been banned, those left with young children face a terrible and devastating decision - turn your babies over to the government or pay the price. For young Freya, keeping her brother hidden is the only real option.

Enemies of the state, Freya must stand between her family and the forces of a fearful world. Although her brother may not be human, there is little else separating her and those of the blue skin.

Choices will be made. Lines will be drawn. The battle for humanity has only just begun.

Available at: www.steven-jenkins.com

Also Available

Eyes On You: A Ghost Story

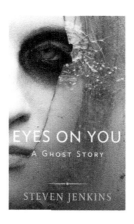

"She's always watching."

Having found the perfect flat, Matthew and Aimee settle into their new home with all the hopes of a young couple in love.

But something hideous resides within its walls.

Before long, curious incidents turn violent, and it becomes increasingly difficult for the sceptic Matthew to deny that an unholy ghost has descended upon his happy home.

Tormented by the wrath of this angry spirit,

Matthew and Aimee's relationship begins to crumble under the weight of their terror, and have no choice but to flee into the night, leaving their beloved flat behind.

But you can never run from your past...because dark secrets have a way of hunting you down.

Available at: www.steven-jenkins.com

Also Available

Burn The Dead: Quarantine
(Book One)

It's a dirty job - but someone's got to do it.

Robert Stephenson burns zombies for a living.

It's an occupation that pays the bills and plays tricks on the mind. Still, his life is routine until his four-year-old son becomes stranded in a quarantined zone, teeming with flesh-eating rotters.

Does Rob have what it takes to fight the undead and put his broken family back together?

Or will he also end up in the incinerator...

Also Available - Burn The Dead: Quarantine

...Burning with the rest of the dead?

Available at: www.steven-jenkins.com

Also Available

Burn The Dead: Purge

(Book Two)

There are those who run, while others hide.

And then, there are the Cleaners.

The living dead have staggered straight out of hell, and all that keeps humanity from crumbling is a small team of men who catch the rotters, before cleaning up the mess left behind.

Catherine Woods might not be a man, but no sexist, out-dated nonsense is going to stop her from following her dreams and joining the war against the undead.

The only problem is—even the best dreams can become nightmares in an instant.

Available at: www.steven-jenkins.com

Also Available

Burn the Dead: Riot
(Book Three)

A sold-out stadium.

A virus unleashed.

For 17-year-old Alfie Button, today was always going to be a memorable day.

The cheers of excited fans soon become desperate, bloodcurdling cries for help as a legion of the undead overwhelms the stadium. Panic erupts as 21,000 people rush for the exits, only to find them sealed.

With nowhere to run, suffocating in a torrent of

blood and chaos, all Alfie and his friends can do is fight for survival—and pray that help will come.

But in every game, in every stadium...

There has to be a loser.

Available at: www.steven-jenkins.com

Also Available

Fourteen Days

Workaholic developer Richard Gardener is laid up at home for two week's mandatory leave—doctor's orders. No stress. No computers. Just fourteen days of complete rest.

Bliss for most, but hell for Richard... in more ways than one. There's a darkness that lives inside Richard's home; a presence he never knew existed because he was seldom there alone.

Did he just imagine those footsteps? The smoke alarm shrieking?

The woman in his kitchen?

His wife thinks that he's just suffering from work

withdrawal, but as the days crawl by in his solitary confinement, the terror seeping through the walls continues to escalate—threatening his health, his sanity, and his marriage.

When the inconceivable no longer seems quite so impossible, Richard struggles to come to terms with what is happening and find a way to banish the darkness—before he becomes an exile in his own home.

Available at: www.steven-jenkins.com

Also Available

Spine:

A Collection of Twisted Tales

Listen closely. A creak, almost too light to be heard...
was it the shifting of an old house, or footsteps down
the hallway? Breathe softly, and strain to hear
through the silence. That breeze against your neck
might be a draught, or an open window.

Slip into the pages of SPINE and you'll be
persuaded to leave the lights on and door firmly
bolted. From Steven Jenkins, bestselling author of
Fourteen Days and *Burn the Dead*, this horror collection of eight stories go beyond the realm of terror to

an entirely different kind of creepiness. Beneath innocent appearances lurk twisted minds and scary monsters, from soft scratches behind the wall, to the paranoia of walking through a crowd and knowing that every single eye is locked on you. In this world, voices lure lost souls to the cliff's edge and illicit drugs offer glimpses of things few should see. Scientists tamper with the afterlife, and the strange happenings at a nursing home are not what they first seem.

So don't let that groan from the closet fool you—the monster is hiding right where you least expect it.

Available at: www.steven-jenkins.com

Also Available

Rotten Bodies:
A Zombie Short Story Collection

We all fear death's dark spectre, but in a zombie apocalypse, dying is a privilege reserved for the lucky few. There are worse things than a bullet to the brain—*much* worse.

Meet Dave, a husband and father with a dirty secret, who quickly discovers that lies aren't only dangerous...they're deadly. Athlete Sarah once ran for glory, but when she finds herself alone on a country road with an injured knee, second place is as good as last. Howard, shovelling coal in the darkness of a Welsh coal mine, knows something's amiss when his colleagues begin to disappear. But it's when the lights come on that things get truly scary.

Five short zombie stories, from the grotesque to the downright terrifying. But reader beware: as the groans get louder and the twitching starts, you'll be *dying* to reach the final page.

Available at: www.steven-jenkins.com

ABOUT THE AUTHOR

Steven Jenkins was born in the small Welsh town of Llanelli, where he began writing stories at the age of eight, inspired by '80s horror movies and novels by *Richard Matheson*.

During Steven's teenage years, he became a great lover of writing dark and twisted poems—six of which gained him publications with *Poetry Now, Brownstone Books*, and *Strong Words*.

Over the next few years, as well as becoming a husband and father, Steven spent his free time writing short stories, achieving further publication with *Dark Moon Digest*. And in 2014 his debut novel, *Fourteen Days* was published by Barking Rain Press.

For More information
www.steven-jenkins.com
author@steven-jenkins.com

.

Printed in Great Britain
by Amazon

21443303R00140